Love And Treachery In Palm Beach 2

Bernard Moran

ISBN: 1523652632
ISBN-13: 9781523652631

Dedicated to Marion, friend and inspiration.

For inspiration and ideas, thanks to Laurie Hosford, Leslie Drew, Tom Leonard and Anne Holt

Special thanks to Marion Ona for format design and computer expertise

Cover design by Jonathan DeLa Rosa

Edited by Sue Alspach

Oh, do not ask, "What is it?"
Let us go and make our visit.

T.S. Eliot

CONTENTS

BREACH OF PROMISE

" --- You know, darling, I'll always love you. There'll never be anyone like you ever again, but I must tell you, and I'm truly sorry, I can't marry you."

Melanie Beasley stared into the eyes of Jamie Cummings with disbelief. This sounded like something from a corny TV soap opera. Her jaw dropped and she started to speak but couldn't.

They were sitting in Taboo and had just finished dinner. It was May in Palm Beach. Melanie and Jamie had planned a June wedding in Atlanta. Melanie came from an old Southern family and considered herself a well-bred lady, but she was known to be hot tempered. There she sat in a public place, a restaurant which Jamie had chosen. He did it on purpose, she thought, because he knew in private there would be an emotional outburst and a loud fight.

"You can't do this to me, Jamie," she said with clenched teeth. "I've already bought my bridal gown and bridesmaids dresses at Joan Pillow, the reception is set for the Piedmont Driving Club, and the wedding is to be held at St. Philips. It's too late to back out."

Jamie tried to clasp her hands, but Melanie pushed him away. "I know this is kind of late in the day to be changing my mind, but honestly, darling, I don't think I'm worthy of you."

What a bunch of BS, Melanie thought. He was weak and she knew it, but she still loved him. If he wanted to back out, she would change his mind. She leaned back in her chair and looked up. "I know marriage is a pretty scary thing these days - so many divorces, so many unhappy people. I think you just have a case of cold feet. Let's talk about this tomorrow."

She noticed Jamie stared at her three-carat diamond engagement ring. Melanie twisted it around her finger. "No, no. I keep the engagement ring no matter what happens." She looked up at him. "You're not in any financial difficulties, are you?"

"No, of course not."

What a silly question, Melanie thought. The Cummings were one of the richest and most prominent families in Atlanta. His family owned the Cummings Manufacturing Company, a maker of plumbing supplies and Jamie worked under his father who was president of the company.

"No, my mind is made up, Melanie. I just don't think I'd make a good husband. You're too fine a person and I don't want to hurt you and make you unhappy."

Jamie's comments stunned Melanie, but she wasn't going to let him go. She knew all his weaknesses - one of which was even though he was rich, he was also tightfisted and found it difficult to part with a buck.

Later that evening she told her mother what happened. She had the same reaction as Melanie - Jamie was weak and was just suffering from nerves. "He'll get over it. He just has to be given time to come around."

Suddenly Melanie stood up. "I've got it, Mom." She started to dance around the room. "Remember the time I was a child, maybe ten or eleven, and we went to see this movie - I can't recall the name of it - and the girl was arguing with her fiance and she threatened him with a breach of promise suit. I'd never heard the expression, breach of promise, so I asked you and dad what it meant. You said she could sue the man for damages if he refused to marry her. Then dad said breach of promise suits were ancient history and didn't exist anymore. The argument continued and got so vehement that those sitting nearby kept shushing you until finally the woman sitting next to you asked you to leave the theater if you couldn't keep quiet. Do you remember the incident?"

"Vaguely, but I think your father was right. Breach of promise suits are a thing of the past."

Melanie gave her mother a searching look. "Why don't we call Mr. McGowan. He's been our family lawyer forever. He should know the answer."

"Well, it's too late now. Let's wait until tomorrow morning."

Melanie tossed all night long. She couldn't believe Jamie had jilted her. It had to be another woman. He was always flirting and his Southern gentleman ways appealed to many women, but why did he tell those stupid lies. He seemed so insincere. Still she loved him and a promise was a promise. He would have to keep his.

The next morning her mother called Mr. McGowan and put the speaker phone on. "Yes, breach of promise is still on the books here in Georgia, though it's rarely used."

Melanie jumped up and down like a jack-in-the-box. "I told you so."

Her mother explained Melanie's predicament.

"Hmm," Mr. McGowan was obviously pondering the situation. "Well, first of all, since you're both Georgia residents and your families are prominent in the community, are you sure you want to do it? The media will have a field day with this."

"Suppose we just threaten to sue," Melanie asked.

"He might give you a cash settlement if that's what you want."

"No. I don't want a cash settlement. I want to marry Jamie Cummings," Melanie shouted into the phone.

"Okay, okay. I'll have to do some research. I know you can sue him for wedding expenses already incurred, but if you're thinking of getting a cash award for humiliation, emotional distress or mental anguish, the courts take a dim view of that today.

"What if we sue for a larger amount, say $200,000? Maybe then he'll come to his senses and do the right thing. Oh, by the way, do I get to keep the engagement ring, Mr. McGowan?"

"Yes, you do. Engagement rings are considered an unconditional gift in the State of Georgia. So no matter what happens, you keep the ring."

They thanked him and said good-bye.

"Invite Jamie to lunch today," her mother said. "Not here. Maybe Green's Pharmacy. Be charming and flirtatious, but don't discuss last night. After lunch walk up to the beach and start talking turkey."

Melanie wore a new dress and a large straw hat. They were cordial to each other at lunch and talked about old times, how they first met at the Harvest Debutante Ball, and how they visited each other often when she was a student at Agnes Scott and he was at Sewanee.

When they arrived at the beach, Melanie removed her shoes, clasped Jamie's hand, and they started to walk in the sand. It was a wonderful Palm Beach day with just a few clouds in the sky and a light ocean breeze.

"You know, Jamie, I thought about what you told me last night and I have to believe you've been cheating on me."

"What makes you think that," he said, and Melanie noticed a slight smile on his face. He has been cheating, she thought. He's always walking around staring at his iPhone. She'd heard about dating sites where women posted photographs of themselves in suggestive poses. Men were such little boys. Well, she could compete with these sluts.

They talked more about the postponed wedding and Jamie agreed reluctantly to reconsider. Melanie suggested they have dinner that night.

After dinner they went back to his house for some passionate sex. She wasn't going to let some cheap Internet whore steal her man, but the next morning Jamie still said he wanted more time to "think things through."

Melanie called Mr. McGowan and told him to overnight paperwork to Jamie, suing him for breach of promise and asking $200,000 as a cash award. Melanie returned to Atlanta and waited for Jamie's reply. Finally after three days she received an overnight letter. It was from Jamie. She climbed the stairs to her bedroom and shut the door.

Sitting down on her bed, her hands started to shake and she put the letter down on the bedspread and said a silent prayer. Cautiously she opened the letter, looked inside and saw a single piece of paper. Pulling it out quickly, she stared at it. It was a check from Jamie for $200,000. She hoped there was a note inside, but there wasn't one.

Melanie threw the check on the floor, removed her engagement ring and hurled it at the wall. Then she sobbed uncontrollably. Her body heaved back and forth. Tears gushed from her eyes. Suddenly she stopped, stood up straight and walked to the window. She stared through the curtains at the garden below. All the flowers were in bloom - roses, hyacinths, peonies, azaleas, and jasmine. It was so beautiful, so peaceful, she thought.

Melanie stopped sobbing and spoke in a loud voice. As someone once said, "I'll think of it all tomorrow. I can stand it then. Tomorrow I'll think of some way to get him back. After all, tomorrow is another day."

AA MEETING

My name is Oliver Michaels and I'm an alcoholic. I have to keep saying this, especially in social situations. It's part of the Alcoholics Anonymous program.

I haven't always been an alcoholic. For years I was just a heavy drinker, but then my life changed.

When I went for my annual checkup Dr. Roberts would say, "Only two drinks per day and no more."

I used to laugh at him. "I have two drinks at lunch, cocktails at six, wine with dinner, and sometimes an after-dinner cordial. How could I only have two drinks per day?"

Then he would say something about if I wanted to have a long life, I should stop drinking completely. I'm only twenty-nine, so I'm not thinking about a long life now - maybe later.

I told him a story my sister related to me. A doctor said to her, "If you don't stop drinking, you'll be dead in five years." But that was ten years ago. The doctor died five years ago and my sister still drinks heavily.

Everybody drinks in Palm Beach unless they are alcoholics like me and go to meetings. I remember when I was younger the time I played bridge with my sister at her home. I had to leave the game early and one of her friends asked me where I was going.

"I have to go to a meeting," I replied. There was silence at the bridge table and the players all exchanged glances.

Finally my sister spoke. "In Palm Beach when you say you're going to a meeting, everyone assumes you're going to an AA meeting." I laughed and assured them I had a meeting with my stockbroker, but the memory of that time lingered.

Recently I went to an AA meeting at the Triangle Club in West Palm Beach. They have meetings in Palm Beach at the Bethesda-By-The-Sea Church, but my sister told me not to go there because I would know most of the attendees. She reminded me in Palm Beach nobody is anonymous. I went to my first meeting reluctantly, but I felt I had to go. Dr. Roberts informed me that my liver was damaged and I had to stop drinking or I would have more serious problems.

I chose to go to the Lunch Bunch meeting held at noon. I was surprised when I arrived. There must have been almost 100 men and women at the meeting; all ages, mainly white, and the majority seemed to be office workers on lunch break.

I'm a lawyer specializing in wills and trusts so I was on my lunch break, too. Ironically the room looked like a perfect place to have a party. Lime green walls, terrazzo floor, and a large gold disco globe in the center of the room. On the walls were posters with AA sayings. "Don't quit before the miracle." "It works if you work it." "Principles before personalities."

I'd heard a lot about AA meetings. It's a support group open to everyone with a desire to stop drinking and a willingness to work the Twelve Step program.

They were working the first step as I walked in, "We admitted that we were powerless over alcohol - that our lives had become unmanageable. I looked around the room and none of the participants had the Palm Beach look except one lady who waved at me as if she knew me.

I put on my glasses and was startled to see my exmother-in-law, Gloria. She was wearing a vintage Pucci red dress with gray accents. Her shoes were Ferragamo black patent leather pumps and she carried a Chanel black purse. I also didn't recognize her because she had had a face lift, a breast augmentation, and her brown hair was dyed blonde. She looked good and about ten years younger than the last time I'd see her.

I sat down next to her and she asked why I was at an AA meeting. I explained and then asked her why she was at the meeting.

I'd seen her about a year previous just before my divorce and I remembered her drinking at that time. She said she'd been an AA member for thirty years, but sometimes she slipped and had a drink.

People around us began to stare and shush us. So we had to stop talking and listen to the individual stories. "Three minutes only," the facilitator said as the tales unfolded.

One man stood up and told his story which seemed almost comical. He said he used to get down on his knees every morning and thank God he'd gone another day without a drink. Now he didn't know what to do because he didn't believe in God anymore and he was afraid he'd start drinking again. "Keep working the program," was the facilitator's advice.

Time began to drag. There were so many attendees not everyone could tell their story. People began to
glance at their watches. Lunch break was almost over
and it was time to get back to work. The meeting ended
with everyone in a circle holding hands and reciting the
Serenity Prayer.

> "God, grant me the serenity to accept the
> things I cannot change; the courage to
> change the things I can; and wisdom to
> know the difference."

Gloria asked me if I would like to join her for lunch.
"Where can we go around here," I asked.

"Downstairs they serve a nice lunch."

We walked down the stairs to what looked like another
party room. On one side was a long cocktail bar, which was
crowded with men and women. I didn't bother to ask if
they served alcohol.

I sat at a table with Gloria and we ordered lunch; tuna
fish sandwiches and Diet Cokes.

"I'm still amazed to see you here. I've seen you take a
drink in social situations, but I've never seen you drunk."

"Well, every now and then I slip up, but I'm usually
under control."

"Do you really feel you need these meetings?"

"Oh, yes, yes, yes. I was a bad girl when I was younger
and I'm afraid of backsliding. Not only did I drink; I smoked
pot and did some hard drugs.

"Really? Your daughter never mentioned this to me
and I never saw her do drugs or get drunk."

"Well, I never told her about my past," Gloria said and smiled coyly.

"I must say you look great."

"Well, I've had some work done," she said with a sly smile. "I suppose you can tell."

"Yes, I can and your surgeon did a great job, but you are all dressed up, turned out as if you're trying to meet a man. Do you think an AA meeting is a good place to meet men?"

Her answer surprised me. "Well, at least we have something in common. I never want to date or marry a drinker."

"That's a good point, but nobody except you looks like they're from Palm Beach."

"Oh, they're here. They're here," she smiled. I've met a few men in the past and even gone out with some."

Interesting. I looked around the room. I didn't see any woman I was attracted to, but unlike Gloria I didn't want to get involved with an ex-drinker.

We finished our lunch and walked upstairs. "It's nice to see you again," Gloria said at the door. "I always liked you and I was sorry when you broke up. I guess you were both too young. By the way, would you like to have a home-cooked meal? You probably eat in restaurants most of the time."

I pondered the question. "Sure. Why not?"

We agreed to meet the following Friday. I wondered if this was a good idea, having dinner with my ex-mother-in-law. I wasn't interested in my ex-wife's life. Since we didn't have children, we never spoke, which was fine by me. We were always fighting when we were married and though Gloria tried to mediate, our marriage was doomed.

I thought about bringing a gift, but what? A bottle of wine? I finally bought a box of Whitman's Sampler chocolates. All alcoholics crave sugar that they aren't getting from alcohol, so it seemed like an appropriate gift.

Gloria lived in a rental apartment on Chilean Avenue. The building was set back from the street and was old and dark, unlike most of the nearby structures. I walked up the outside stairs to her apartment and knocked on the door. I heard soft music playing inside and the lights were dim.

Finally Gloria opened the door. "Come on in, she said. Her words were slurred and I could smell alcohol on her breath. She turned and started to walk with an unsteady gait. She wore lavender shorts, a pink halter top, and flip-flops. She turned and stood by the couch.

"Have a seat," she said pointing. I was taken aback by this unexpected scene. At first I wasn't sure what to do. Finally I put the chocolates on the couch, knelt down on the floor, and started to repeat in a loud voice: "God, grant me the serenity to accept the things I cannot change; the courage to change the things I can; and wisdom to know the difference."

THE EXPATS

Donald Mayfield awoke in a sweat, his pajama top soaked and his hair matted. It was that scary dream again. He was in an amateur play and it was opening night. He had taken his script to the theater so he could study it because he wasn't sure he knew his lines and he was terrified he'd miss a cue or forget one of his speeches, but when he reached the theater he couldn't find his script.

He searched frantically backstage; first in the green room, then where the costumes hung, and finally on the prop desk. He still couldn't find it. He thought about going out into the theater to look, but the audience had started to arrive. He asked other cast members if he could borrow their scripts, but they had left them at home.

Then he woke up. It was all so real, so vivid, so terrifying. Donald knew what the dream meant. Even though he'd only performed once in a play and that was forty years ago when he was a student at Choate and had a small part in *The Man Who Came to Dinner*.

No, this wasn't about make-believe. This was about life, his life, which was a maze of confusion. Ever since his wife Eve died just over a year ago he felt lost. She had been his anchor and now he was adrift.

He'd lived with his wife in Palm Beach for ten years, ever since he retired from J.P. Morgan as a trust officer. They loved Palm Beach - the radiant sky, the aqua blue ocean, the friends, the golf, the parties. They really enjoyed themselves.

Since her death he played golf on occasion, but without enthusiasm. He was no longer interested in the social scene. Friends tried to match him with women, but he always declined. He told them he was still grieving.

The truth was that he wasn't interested in feminine companionship and all sexual desire had vanished. This worried him because he was only sixty-five and he felt that he should be interested in sex.

He didn't seem to know how to use his time. Most days he sat in Green's Pharmacy and watched and listened. Green's was the Broadway and 42nd Street of Palm Beach. Sooner or later everyone in Palm Beach came to Green's; socialites to fill prescriptions and buy cosmetics, tourists to buy sundries and items for the beach, workers to have lunch.

Green's was comfortable - an old-fashioned drugstore that still had a luncheonette. The food was good and the waitresses called most of the customers by their first name or just "honey."

Donald not only watched, he listened to the conversations. One day he heard two older men discussing Costa Rica. They felt it was the place to go if you wanted sex with younger women. Prostitution was legal and so was gambling. Jaco Beach, a resort town, was only seventy miles from San Jose, the capitol, and there were many American expats who lived there.

Why not, Donald thought. Anything to forget his wife and rekindle his sexual desire. That night he Googled Costa Rica and learned there were nonstop three-hour flights from Fort Lauderdale for only about $250 round trip. He also learned the place to stay was the Del Rey Casino and the casino's Blue Marlin Bar was the spot to find women. If he tired of San Jose, he could always drive to Jaco Beach.

It was February, the height of the social season in Palm Beach, and a good time to get away, Donald thought.

Donald walked into the Blue Marlin Bar and was surprised. There must have been over a hundred men and women crowded around the oblong bar placed in the middle of the room. The men all seemed to be senior Americans and the women Costa Ricans in their twenties. Most were Hispanic-looking with dark hair and olive skin. Some were blond and blue-eyed and a few showed Indian heritage. All were well-groomed and well-dressed and appeared eager to do business.

"Good evening, sir. Care to buy me a drink," several women asked as Donald circled the bar. He stopped to talk to one of the women because she spoke English with only the slightest accent and she was prettier than the others.

"What will you have," Donald asked. She requested a Scotch and soda and Donald ordered a Cognac. They touched glasses and Donald asked her if she was here every night.

"No, only occasionally," she replied. "I work as a secretary during the day and I'm usually too tired."

Donald had heard that the women were tested monthly for venereal diseases and thought if she wasn't at the Blue Marlin every night she might be disease free.

They talked briefly about his life in Palm Beach. She told him her name was Ingrid and her parents had emigrated from Germany to Costa Rica after World War II. Then she suggested they go back to his room.

Taken aback by her bluntness, he managed to blurt out, "How much?"

"A hundred dollars for an hour."

"Hm-mmm. How about fifty," he replied.

They agreed to the price and Ingrid downed her drink. "Let's go," she said.

Very businesslike, he thought, but of course this was a business transaction. He opened the door to his room and turned on the light.

"Care for a drink?"

Ingrid shook her head and sat on the bed.

"I think I'll have one," Donald said, filling his water glass with Cognac. He hoped the drink would increase his desire.

"Do you want me to take my clothes off?"

"No, no. That's okay. Let's talk for a while."

Ingrid looked at her watch and frowned.

"You know, you remind me of some American women I know." Actually, she reminded him of some of his American relatives and he wished he hadn't thought of that. He couldn't have sex with someone who reminded him of his relatives.

Ingrid smiled at him in an inviting manner. He knew this was the time to act, but he couldn't or wouldn't.

"Let me pay you now," he said. "Here's a fifty and another fifty as a tip. Let's talk some more." He took a long gulp of his drink and started to tell Ingrid why he'd come to Costa Rica.

She seemed interested, but he couldn't be sure she was listening.

"I just had enough of Palm Beach and I was looking for a change. I don't know if Costa Rica is for me, but I'm going to find out. Do you have a boyfriend?"

"Not at the moment, but when I stop this kind of work I guess I'll find one and get married. I'm hoping to save a lot of money before I get married."

"For your dowry?"

"No, no," she laughed. We don't have dowries anymore in Costa Rica, but secretaries salaries are low here.

Donald felt tired from the flight. This was a mistake. He should have waited until tomorrow when he felt stronger.

Ingrid slipped her clothes off and laid back on the bed. The time to talk had ended.

"Care to join me," she asked and beckoned him toward the bed. He stared at her naked body. It was beautiful and young and fresh and clean, but he felt no desire. He put his hand in his pants pocket and felt his penis. It was soft and small.

He now had two choices. He could lie down beside her and hope for an erection after some foreplay, or just forget about having sex. Even though Donald always tried to get good value for his money, he decided not to try.

"I'm sorry," he said. "You know, I just got off the plane this afternoon. I guess I should have waited until tomorrow."

"That's okay," she said sitting up in bed. She dressed quickly and walked towards him. "I'll be in the casino tomorrow night. Maybe we can try it again."

She kissed him on the cheek and walked towards the door. There's no fool like an old fool, he thought.

The next day he packed his bag and checked out. He'd had enough of San Jose and wanted to try Jaco Beach. He settled on a price with a cab driver for a one-way and a round-trip fare. He wasn't sure whether he'd stay over or come back to San Jose.

It was a nice drive down the highway. He relaxed and talked with the driver. Donald told him he wanted to meet some American expats and the driver assured him he knew exactly the place to go.

Along the drive there wasn't much to see, but when they arrived in Jaco Donald was surprised. Not only was Jaco a thriving beach resort with hotels, motels, and condos lining the beach, but it was Americanized. They passed Kentucky Fried Chicken, McDonald's, and other fast-food restaurants.

The cab pulled up at a bar called, ironically, Gringos located fifty yards from the beach. Donald noticed the waves, large breakers that rolled in towards the shore; Pacific waves, like the ones in California, not like the small Atlantic waves that crashed on the beach back home. However, the sand was brown and the beach strewn with trash. It was before noon when they walked in the bar, but the noise was loud.

Most of the patrons were American men dressed in shorts and sandals. Some sat at tables with gaudily-dressed women who Donald assumed were prostitutes.

"Hi, Yank. Welcome to Jaco," one of the men at the bar said to Donald as he walked in. "Can I buy you a drink?"

"This round is on me," Donald replied. He wanted information from these men about Jaco.

"I'm Ken," the man said shaking hands. His voice was raspy and his eyes were bloodshot. He hadn't shaved in at least two days.

Ken introduced his buddies and Donald ordered a round of beers. "How do you like it here," he asked.

"I love it. I've got my friends. We meet every day here. And if I want to get laid, I don't have to look very far." He glanced over at the tables.

"What do you do when you're not here - play golf, go swimming?"

"Nah. We spend most of our time here."

Donald was surprised by his answer. Ken looked like he might have been an executive back in the States.

"Where are you from," Donald asked.

"Milwaukee. I did thirty years as an executive with AT&T and then I retired here five years ago."

"What about your family?"

"What about them? I'm divorced. My son and daughter and grandchildren all live in Milwaukee."

"Don't you miss them?"

"No. Every time I see them, all they do is ask me for money. I told them not to ask anymore because I was going to spend all my money in Costa Rica. I also told them that I hope the last check that I write in my life will bounce."

This comment was followed by loud laughter by Ken and his friends. Donald was not amused. Lotus eaters, he thought, living an idle life of selfishness and dissipation. Although he felt sorry for Ken and his buddies, he had to admit they seemed happy.

"This lifestyle is unhealthy. You're not going to live long doing this every day."

"So what," Ken replied. "Look, I'm living my life the way I want to. I did my time with AT&T and now I'm going to party hearty until I drop. As I told you, my family only wants my money and they're not going to get it."

Donald said good-bye and left. "I think I've seen enough of Costa Rica," he told the cab driver. "Take me to the airport."

He thought about his wife and how much he missed her, dead at fifty-seven though she had led such a healthy, exemplary life. It just wasn't fair, but he knew as everyone knew that life wasn't fair. Now he felt only contempt for Ken and his buddies - throwing their lives away.

He thought of Palm Beach and all his friends who tried to help him mourn his wife Eve. Maybe it was time to get active again. He had his charities to work on. He could still play golf.

And if he wasn't ready for the party social scene, he might at least start dating again. He could put the past behind him, live in the present, and look toward the future. His children might not need his financial help, but they appreciated his wisdom and experience; and he was absolutely sure Eve wouldn't want him to be so alone.

WHERE THERE'S A WILL THERE'S A RELATIVE

Mark Hubbard was bored with looking at his late mother's estate personal property list. She had died a month earlier and it was time to divide her belongings among the heirs, but there was nothing Mark wanted. Furniture, jewelry, paintings, objets d'art - the usual things found in a Palm Beach home.

All of the items had been appraised, catalogued and given a dollar value, but Mark knew the appraised value was retail and if he tried to sell the object, he would receive half the stated value.

He handed the list to his girlfriend Michelle LaFleur with whom he shared his one-bedroom City Place apartment.

"Do you see anything on this list you like?"

Michelle flipped through the pages and laughed. "What's this? A Louis XVI style mahogany and beechwood commode?"

Mark sighed. "A commode is a chest of drawers, not a toilet."

Michelle seemed surprised. Originally from Atlanta, her real name was Wanda Grabowski. She changed it because she felt Michelle LaFleur was more stylish. She worked in women's wear at Neiman Marcus, Worth Avenue and hoped one day to own her own boutique.

"I think we should concentrate on gold and silver items," Mark said. "Both metals are down right now, but long-term they should go higher. Besides, you can always sell gold and silver. Furniture and jewelry can be difficult to sell."

"Here's something interesting. An 18-carat gold Tiffany & Co. eight-piece dresser set," Michelle said.

"But it's monogrammed HAH, Harriet Ames Hubbard, my mother's initials, which will make it hard to sell."

"What about this - two Tiffany & Co. fourteen-carat yellow gold nut dishes in a square-flared design?"

"They look interesting. I'll bid on them."

"What do you mean, bid on them?"

"On advice of the estate's lawyer when we meet to divide the estate, we use a deck of playing cards. All three of us, my sister and my brother, will pick a card. Say my number is nine. An item is then selected and mother's maid Shirley will turn the cards over. If my number comes up, I can select the item or pass on it. If an item comes up that two of us want, then we can bid above the stated value and the highest bidder gets it."

Michelle looked confused. "Sounds complicated."

"Not really."

"Can I go to this party?"

"Sorry. Only the three of us. No husbands, wives, girlfriends, boyfriends, or significant others."

"What about cash?"

"There's no cash in the estate. We found out mother took out a reverse mortgage on the house and lived for years off the proceeds."

"How about all her jewelry she used to flaunt?"

"All fake. At one point she had some expensive pieces, but she sold them all and bought fakes. The estate is worth a little over $300,000. So we each have a share of about $100,000."

"That's all?"

"Afraid so."

"What about your mother's clothes and all those ball gowns?"

"They don't have much resale value."

Michelle continued to flip the pages. "What about art works?"

"I don't know. I guess some of the paintings are valuable. I don't know much about the current art market."

Suddenly Michelle stood up. "This is interesting, 'A Vision of the Grand Canal' by Felix Ziem."

"Yeah, I've been looking at that all my life. What's it appraised at?"

"$25,000."

"Well, I guess it's worth it. I don't know if we can sell it at that price."

Michelle became excited. "I'm sure I saw a similar painting at My Favorite Things - you know, that gallery on Worth Avenue."

"Do you think it was painted by Ziem?"

"I do. I really do and it was listed at $150,000."

Mark sat up. "Are you sure?"

"Yes, I'm positive about the price and pretty sure it was Ziem."

Mark grabbed the list from Michelle and looked at the black-and-white photograph. He ran to his desk, opened his laptop, and Googled Felix Ziem. "Let's see what we've got here."

Mark studied the paintings of Ziem on his computer. "I think you've hit on something, Michelle. If you're right and I win the bid, we can resell it. Even if we can't get $150,000, we can surely get more than $25,000. Look at this," he said getting excited. "In 2009 Ziem's painting 'The Golden Horn' sold for $302,144."

"Oh, my God. We've struck it rich." Michelle danced around the living room.

"Hold on, hold on," Mark said trying to calm her down. "This painting is 52 by 85 1/2. That's gigantic. Very few rooms would be big enough for that sized painting. It must have been bought by a museum."

Mark looked up from his laptop. "Does the list give the dimensions of mother's painting?"

"Yes. 21 by 33 1/4."

"Well, that's a better size for a living room." Mark stood up. "You know, I think we should drive over to My Favorite Things right now."

Mark went into the bedroom to change. He put on his pink polo shirt, khaki Bermuda shorts with a Vineyard Vines belt, and Gucci loafers.

"What's this," Michelle asked when he walked back into the living room.

"My Palm Beach outfit."

"Well, I'm not going to change," she replied.

Michelle wore a blue tank top, white short shorts and flip-flops. With high cheek bones, slanty brown eyes and long tightly curled hair, she was attractive in an exotic way.

While driving to Palm Beach Mark mused about the painting and how it might change his life. If he could sell it for $150,000 or thereabouts, he could give up his job as a waiter and open up the boutique Michelle always talked about. Then he could be his own boss for a change. Well, sort of. Michelle would actually be the boss - he knew nothing about women's wear, but they'd be partners.

Mark worked as a waiter only to save money so they could open the boutique. At first he worked at many of the Palm Beach restaurants - Mike McCarty's, Palm Beach Grill, Testa's, the Colony, even the Breakers, but he kept seeing diners he knew and it embarrassed him to be seen as a waiter. There were many twenty and thirty-something waiters in Palm Beach who had gone to New England prep schools and colleges, but these were temporary positions, not career jobs.

Mark was forty-five and looked it. His hair, what there was of it, was mostly gray and he had developed a paunch.

Now he worked in West Palm Beach restaurants because of an incident that happened over a year ago. His history teacher from Hotchkiss, Mr. Hertz, saw Mark at Mike McCarty's and started the conversation with, "Oh, how the mighty are fallen."

What a pompous ass, Mark felt like saying.

"I remember you as an A student and someone who wanted to teach history," he continued with a frown.

Mark countered with his familiar tale about owning his own restaurant and marrying his girlfriend.

"Is this pathetic tale supposed to garner sympathy and perhaps a large tip? If so, it's falling on deaf ears."

What a bastard, Mark thought. He resigned that night from Mike McCarty's.

Mark stepped inside My Favorite Things and smiled. He spoke to an elderly woman who he assumed owned the store. "Hi. I'm Mark Hubbard. I think you knew my mother Harriet Hubbard."

"Oh, yes," her manner softened. Then she glared at Michelle in a disapproving way. "I was sorry to hear of her passing. A very great lady. How may I be of service?"

He explained about the Ziem painting and asked if she had sold any Ziems lately.

"Yes, as a matter of fact we had two of his paintings here last year and sold both of them."

"May I ask the price of the paintings?"

The woman shook her head. We never divulge the price of anything we sell here. If you have a Ziem, I would certainly like to see it and perhaps we can consign it."

Mark explained that he didn't own the painting as yet, but when he did he would bring it into the store. He thanked the saleswoman and then left with Michelle.

"I think we should go over to Christie's and find out what they have to say about Ziem. They are a big art auction house."

They walked in and were greeted by a tall blonde with an affected accent. She ignored Michelle and smiled at Mark. He explained about the Ziem painting.

"Let me check my computer. Has it been sold recently?"

"No. It's been in the family for over 100 years and as far as I know my great-grandfather bought it soon after it was painted."

"Good. So it has no provenance, which means it has no known value and might be worth more than some of his other Venice paintings."

Mark described the size of the painting and the subject matter.

The woman said, "Ziem was famous for painting the Grand Canal in Venice. He probably painted it fifty times. I would think it might be worth $70,000. Maybe more."

She handed him a card that listed Christie's standard selling charges. He read it quickly and was surprised. "Wow, you guys certainly take a big cut."

She shrugged her shoulders. "There's also an insurance charge, a shipping fee, a catalogue illustration fee, and possibly a ten percent administration charge." She sounded bored as if she were talking to a school boy who knew nothing of art.

"Well, let me think about it," Mark replied lamely and left.

On the way out Michelle looked at him sharply. "Look, the first order of business is to get the painting when you guys meet to divide the estate."

"Don't worry," Mark said with clenched teeth. "And remember there are also local consigners who won't charge as much."

Mark burst through the door of his apartment. "I've got it. I've got it," he shouted.

"How much did you have to pay?"

"$35,000. My sister wanted it, but I outbid her." He ripped off the brown wrapping paper and placed it on the floor. "What do you think," he said.

"Well, I'm no expert, but I think it looks good. Let's Google paintings of the Grand Canal and see what comes up?" Michelle stared intently at her laptop.

"Wow, for an artist I've never heard of, he sure seems popular. Look at all these sites. Here's one that offers copies of Ziem paintings at a reduced price."

"Find a site that shows Grand Canal paintings," Mark said with impatience.

"Here it is," Michelle said looking at her laptop. "Look at all these sales. The majority sold for between $80,000 and $100,000. Maybe we can get more because ours was sold only once and has no provenance.

Mark turned and looked at the Ziem he had placed against the wall. It was signed at the lower right-hand side and had a small plaque on the frame with Ziem's name on it. The painting was dominated by a large sailboat which had a blue and white diagonal sail with a red pennant that fluttered from the mast.

"I think it compares favorably with those online paintings," he said.

"Let's get an opinion."

Mark removed a piece of paper from his pocket. "I have the names of some local art experts. Let's see what they have to say."

They drove south to Olive Avenue and reached West Palm Beach Appraisers.

"Let's leave the painting in the car," Mark said. "We want to make sure these guys are legit."

Mark banged hard on the door. Then he heard the locks click open.

"What do you want," someone shouted in a gruff voice without opening the door.

"We want to consign a painting," Mark shouted.

Finally the door open and a man dressed in jeans and sandals stood before Mark. "Come in," he said tentatively. The man had a full salt-and-pepper beard, curly hair and wore spectacles.

Mark looked around in the dim light. It was a large warehouse with high ceilings and TV screens placed overhead. Furniture, paintings and bric-a-brac were placed in home-like settings.

"What have you got," the man said. He still seemed suspicious.

Mark replied, "A Felix Ziem painting of the Grand Canal."

"Oh, sure," the man brightened. "I know Ziem. We've sold his work before. My name is Bruce Cogar." He smiled and shook Mark's hand.

"How do things work around here," Mark asked.

"Well, we've joined the 21st century. Every month we hold an auction here at the warehouse, but it's also online so we have buyers from all over the world." Bruce became more animated as he talked. "No, we're not Christie's or Sotheby's, but our buyers have money."

"How much do you charge," Mark interrupted.

"Well, it's negotiable, but usually around twelve percent."

"What about photography for the catalogue?"

"A one-time $100 photography charge and since we do the selling here, you don't have to pay shipping, insurance, and there's no processing fee."

"Sounds good." Mark looked over at Michelle and she nodded. He continued, "The painting is in the car. I'll go get it."

Bruce took the painting into his glass-enclosed office and showed it to an associate who first looked at the painting closely with a hand magnifier. Then he took a jeweler's loupe and examined it more closely and said something to Bruce.

Mark tried to read his lips, but couldn't.

Bruce opened the door and smiled strangely at Mark and Michelle. Mark sensed something was amiss when Bruce invited them into his office and asked them to sit. "Care for a cup of coffee or perhaps tea?"

"No, thanks," Mark answered quickly. Something was definitely wrong, Mark thought. He could feel the sweat under his arms.

"How long did you say this painting was in your family?"

The question seemed odd. "Over 100 years. My great-grandfather bought it before I was born and I remember seeing it all my life."

"Hmm." Bruce seemed pensive. He quickly typed into his computer, waited a few second, then swung the screen around towards Mark who stared at the screen and stood.

"That's the same painting as mine," he said and pointed. "I don't get it."

"I'm sorry to inform you," Bruce said, trying to comfort. "This painting was sold six years ago at auction in Sotheby's in New York."

Bruce was stunned. "Then what's my painting," he asked in a weak voice.

"It's a fake. A good one, but nevertheless a fake. Whoever owned this painting must have sold the original and then had someone forge the painting you brought in."

Mark remembered ruefully that Michelle had mentioned an internet site which sold Ziem copies.

"Are you absolutely positive it's a fake?" Mark had trouble saying the words.

"I'm sure," Bruce replied. "My colleague who is a trained Morellian expert just looked at it. He's positive it's a forgery."

Mark slumped in his chair, his mouth agape. "Well, well," he stammered and looked at Michelle.

"A well is a hole in the ground," she said and smiled at him sweetly.

MALE MENOPAUSE

Hobart Means stepped outside his cabana at the Poinsettia Club into the bright sunlight and blinked.

"Hi, Mr. Means. How are you?"

The voice sounded youthful and eager, but he couldn't place it. He put his hand over his eyes to block the sun and stared at the girl before him. Dressed in a tiny pink bikini with a matching wide-brimmed straw hat, she looked gorgeous.

"I'm Holly Syms. Don't you remember me," she said.

"Of course, of course," he replied flustered. "You've grown up. I remember you as a little girl splashing around in the pool. It seems like only yesterday."

"Well, I'm home on Spring Break from Foxcroft and next fall I'm going to Brown."

"Wow, time sure flies, doesn't it? Well, congratulations."

Hobart felt a stiffness between his legs and moved his towel to the front of his swimsuit. He hadn't felt this sort of sexual excitement in a long time. He thought of his wife Fran. He couldn't remember the last time they had sex. They were the same age, fifty-six. Clearly she was no longer interested in sex and Hobart felt the same. But now seeing Holly, he was aroused in a way he thought no longer possible. It's not me; it's Fran, he thought.

He sat by the pool and looked around. He watched the men and women as they walked to the dining pavilion. Most of them were middle-aged or older and it occurred to Hobart there were two types of women at the Poinsettia Club; the slender ones with pinched leathery faces, given to broad-brimmed hats, Bermuda shorts and Capezio flats, and the other type were the frowsie-blowsies with their scarlet faces, long caftans and hairnets.

He thought he was too critical of the women and pondered how he looked. His thinning hair was gray, his face fleshy, and his jawline barely perceptible, his stomach pressed against his pants and he had let his belt out three notches. No, he wasn't the answer to every maiden's prayer, not that he knew any maidens except Holly Syms.

Still, if Holly could arouse him, maybe it was time for a makeover if he wanted to test his desirability. A facelift and a hair-coloring should take ten years off the way he looked. The hair-coloring was easy. The guy who cut his hair could do that.

But plastic surgery? He couldn't have it done in Palm Beach. Everyone would know. Miami would be a good place. He would tell Fran he was on a business trip. She wouldn't ask any questions.

He went online and typed in "Plastic Surgeons Miami" and found a very long list. The one called Elysian Fields had such an amusing name. So Hobart called them and asked to come in for a consultation.

When he arrived at the clinic on Brickell Avenue he was surprised how large it was. Located in a high-rise building, it took up almost the entire fifth floor.

The receptionist greeted him and took him into a small adjoining room. Soon the doctor arrived. He was stylishly dressed in a light gray suit that matched the color of the walls. He introduced himself as Tibor Nemeth. He spoke with a thick Hungarian accent and was extremely gracious.

"Mr. Means," he said as he pulled the skin around his jaw, "I think we have to take a tuck here and, of course, we have to do the eyelids, upper and lower. I'll have my assistant type up a proposal while you wait in the reception area."

Hobart walked out into the waiting room. The receptionist, a middle-aged woman, smiled at him.

"Dr. Nemeth really does good work," she said. "Look what he did for me. My eyes were sagging and my neck was like crepe paper."

She pulled out a hand mirror from her desk drawer and admired herself. "I can't recommend him highly enough."

Hobart was suspicious. She didn't look that youthful and he wondered if she told all the potential patients the same story.

Presently a woman in a white coat entered and ushered him into an adjoining room. She opened a folder and handed him a typed paper. He read it and couldn't believe his eyes. Talk about sticker shock! The proposal was for $18,500.

"I know it seems expensive," the woman said, "But Dr. Nemeth is world famous for his work."

Hobart looked at the itemized prices. He still couldn't believe it. $9,000 for a face-neck platysmaplasty, lower eyelids blepharoplasty $3,000, upper eyelids blepharoplasty

$2,000, anesthesia and facility fees $4,500 - it seemed outrageous.

"Is Dr. Nemeth's work guaranteed," he asked in an aggressive voice.

"Well, we take photographs before and after the procedures and you can see for yourself the difference. We can't guarantee doctor's work, but I can show you before-and-after photos of other patients, if you want."

She opened a loose-leaf binder and Hobart looked at some of the photos. He was impressed.

"How soon can we do the procedure," he asked.

"I can make an appointment right now, sir."

She opened a large book. "How about June 10th at 2:00 p.m.?"

"That sounds good."

Fran would be at their summer home in Easthamptom, the club would be closed for the season, and most of their friends would be away. He would soon find out if he could still attract younger women.

"How long before the stitches are removed?"

"Usually about two weeks."

"That would be toward the end of June. Fine. Let's do it."

After the stitches were removed, Hobart stared at himself in his bathroom mirror. He thought he looked at least ten years younger. The bags under his eyes were gone and the skin had been tightened around his jawline. It was time to test his younger look on younger women.

He dressed carefully in a blue button-down shirt with the sleeves rolled to the elbows, designer jeans and Bass loafers. On his wrist he wore his gold Rolex Oyster Perpetual watch and on his right hand his gold signet ring with the Means coat-of-arms.

His tinted brown hair was combed over the bald spot at the back of his head. At the sides to hide his receding hairline the hair was combed down.

Rick's in West Palm Beach was the current choice to find available women. Modeled after Humphrey Bogart's bar in Casablanca, it was the newest in-spot.

The valet parked his BMW 750 sedan and Hobart walked in. On his left was a life-like figure of Bogart dressed in a white dinner jacket and on his right Ingrid Bergman in a white suit. Faux palm trees were placed strategically around the room and next to the bar was a dance floor with a small band playing. As in the movie, there was a white upright piano and as Hobart sat down at the bar, the band started to play *As Time Goes By*.

Before his Mojito was served, two women sat beside him. They looked to be in their late twenties, stylishly coiffed and attired. One was blond and the other brunette. Both had deep suntans.

"Can I buy you a drink," Hobart offered.

"No, that's okay," the blond answered.

They both ordered Metropolitans.

Hobart was miffed his offer had been refused, but unlike when he was in his twenties he knew women preferred to buy their own drinks.

"Do you come here often," he asked when the drinks were served.

"Not really. How about yourself?"

"This is my first time. It's quite a place. Now if only Sidney Greenstreet and Peter Lorre would appear."

They all chuckled. Hobart introduced himself and they told him they were Sally and Betsy Steele. They both worked as associates at Chez Marie's Boutique in City Place.

"How about a dance," Hobart asked and led the blond to the dance floor. He held her close as the band played *Just One of Those Things*. He felt her cheek against his and her body pressed tightly against him. "This is going to be easy," he thought. "I guess the makeover worked."

The song ended and he returned the woman to the bar and then led her sister onto the floor. The band played *Anything Goes*, and once again he held the woman close to him.

Drinks and dancing continued for about an hour. The women seemed eager for anything. Hobart suggested they all go back to his place for a nightcap.

"Why not our place," Sally suggested. "We live nearby."

"Let's do it," Hobart replied.

The valet brought his car around and Hobart followed the girls to their apartment in City Place.

"This is a beautiful pad you've got here," Hobart said as he stretched out on the sofa.

"What will you have to drink," Sally asked.

"Well, if you can't make a Mojito, rum and tonic with a lime."

Hobart excused himself and went to the bathroom. When he returned his drink was on the coffee table. The girls sat on either side of him and they toasted.

Hobart nervously took a long sip from his drink. It had been over thirty years since he'd been in a woman's apartment. He wondered what was going to happen next.

He sighed and laid back on the couch. The two women sat closer. He placed his arms around both of them and tilted his head to the right to kiss Sally. Her face seemed blurred.

"You look ..." He tried to speak, but couldn't. He tried to stand up, but his muscles wouldn't work. Putting his head back on the couch, he closed his eyes.

All of a sudden he was back at Yale and it was a fall football weekend. Yale had beaten Princeton and Hobart had taken his weekend date, Ginny Matthews, first to Mory's for dinner and then to the Fence Club for a dance. Back at her room in the Taft Hotel, he'd undressed her and they had just gotten into bed. He had waited for this all day. He started to caress her. What a beautiful moment this would be.

He felt someone shake him and shine a flashlight in his face.

A voice asked, "Are you alright?"

Hobart rubbed his eyes and looked up. It was a Palm Beach police officer. Hobart saw the ocean in front of him. He was sitting in his car, but on the passenger's side.

"Where am I? What happened?"

The officer smiled. "You're near Peruvian Avenue, it's 3:00 a.m., and there's no overnight parking here, sir."

Hobart reached in his pocket. His wallet was gone. He looked at his hands. His watch and ring were missing. He rubbed his eyes and tried to remember what happened. The officer was still smiling.

"I met these two women at Rick's ..."

"And they invited you back to their apartment for a drink. Then you went to the bathroom and they slipped a roofie in your drink."

Hobart stared at the officer. "A what?"

"A roofie. Probably rohypnol - they're called date rape drugs, though I don't think you were raped."

Hobart sat up straight in his seat. The officer was beginning to irritate him. "Well, I'd like to press charges," he huffed.

"Do you remember the girls' names?"

He scratched his head. "No, I don't."

"Well, you can't very well press charges then. If you want, I can file a report but then it might appear in the newspapers. Would you like that?"

The officer was insufferable. "No, I don't think so."

What a fool I've been, he thought. Well, at least no one will know about it.

"Shall I call a cab or can you give me a ride home," he asked the officer meekly.

WEDDING BELL REDS

Sylvia Hutchins was of a singular mind to marry off her only daughter Melanie. Unfortunately Melanie had a "past," not the familiar Palm Beach past of sexual adventures and abortions or the other Palm Beach favorite, cocaine and heroin abuse. Melanie's past was somewhat unusual. As a teenager she was overweight and a diet doctor prescribed pep pills to speed up her metabolism and help her slim down.

Unfortunately Melanie became addicted and started to buy "reds," street uppers. She became so hyperactive that she had to buy street downers to sleep. The combination of uppers and downers drove Melanie to a nervous collapse, which took her two years to recover from. After insulin and shock therapy she was still somewhat fuzzy mentally and couldn't remember past events. Her excess weight returned and her self-confidence ebbed.

Sylvia felt guilt and partial responsibility for Melanie's plight and vowed to see her wed to an appropriate man. But who? Melanie was now twenty-nine, still eligible by current standards, but suitors were rare or unacceptable.

Almost everyone was married at the Bougainvillea Club, so that was an unlikely place to look. Melanie worked at Winston-Croydon, a Worth Avenue men's store, which seemed like a good place to meet potential suitors, but so far it had produced no results.

Sylvia thought about her daughter's predicament often. She solicited friends' advice in hopes they might suggest someone suitable, but most of them shrugged and reminded her that marriage was not as popular as it was in their day.

Sylvia was not daunted by her friends' negativity. She tried other approaches. She scanned Melanie's Palm Beach Day School yearbook and Googled anyone who looked possible. She tried online dating sites and the Social Register, but they proved useless. She wanted to find a man who lived in Palm Beach and hopefully one who grew up in Palm Beach - somebody who knew the rules and had similar values.

Melanie told her mother that she was dating a man who worked as a salesman at the store. He was from Riviera Beach so Sylvia didn't consider him marriage material. She assumed Melanie felt as she did. At least she was back in circulation again and though he wasn't eligible, at least he was an admirer.

But Melanie surprised Sylvia by asking him to a family dinner. A widow, Sylvia invited a friend, Lawrence Foley, to join them. Lawrence was known as "Mr. Palm Beach" though there were others who claimed the title. He was handsome, a good dancer, with a sparkling wit, and a favored escort at cocktail parties and charity balls.

Sylvia lived in a large home in the estate section, a home which had been in the family for fifty years, not an original Mizner but a large Spanish-styled pink stucco home.

Melanie had not discussed Leland with her mother, so Sylvia didn't know what to expect, but she thought if he lived in Riviera Beach he had no education, no money, no class. Sylvia was surprised when they arrived for cocktails and Melanie introduced Leland.

"Very pleased to meet you, ma'am," he replied in a deep Southern accent, something rarely heard in Palm Beach. He was dressed in a dark gray suit, blue button-down shirt, striped tie, and Cordovan Oxford shoes. Very business-like, Sylvia thought, but they probably came directly from the store.

He was handsome in a rugged sort of way; strong jaw line with a cleft chin, black wavy hair, and deep brown eyes. He was not at all what she expected. He seemed so poised, so composed, so comfortable. She thought he would be intimidated by the sumptuous surroundings, but he wasn't. She also noticed how attentive Melanie was and how she listened intently when he spoke and stared at him constantly.

"It's so nice to have young people for dinner. Lawrence and I are so used to being with older folks," Sylvia said, trying to put Leland at ease. "How long have you been working at Winston-Croydon?"

"About two years, ma'am. I started right after I got out of the Army."

"Oh, you must have been in Afghanistan."

"How was it," Lawrence asked.

Leland hesitated. "Well, my dad's a career Army man and served thirty years. He retired as a master sergeant. I was somewhat skeptical about enlisting, but dad convinced me it was the right thing to do. I had even thought about making it a career, but I guess I saw too much. Frankly I was happy to get home."

"I served in Viet Nam, another unpopular war. So I know how you feel," Lawrence said.

"Did you ever think of becoming an officer," Sylvia asked.

Melanie gave her an angry look.

"My dad said he could get me an appointment to West Point if I was interested, but my math grades were low and I don't think I would have been accepted."

"But why work in a men's store? It seems unusual after being in the Army," Lawrence wondered.

"My uncle is the store manager and he felt we might open our own store in Riviera Beach after I got some experience."

Why not Worth Avenue, Sylvia thought. I could lend or even give him the money. She couldn't believe she had such ideas. She had just met this man and though he certainly was polite and presentable, she wondered if he was appropriate for Melanie; and anyhow he hadn't yet asked her to marry him.

She looked at both of them intently. They didn't make for an attractive couple. He really was handsome in a strong masculine way, with erect posture and healthy-looking eyes and skin. Melanie slumped in her chair, her skin was pasty, her hair dull and her dress loose-fitting to hide her weight problem. Sylvia was in a quandary. She had been prepared to dislike or dismiss this man as an inappropriate admirer, but now she thought Melanie was lucky to have him.

"Dinner is served," the maid announced and they all walked into the dining room. Hilda, their maid, was dressed in a formal uniform, a black dress with white lace collar, a matching apron and cap. The table was set with four silver candlesticks placed on a white lace runner with a silver centerpiece filled with orchids. Each place setting had three forks, two knives, two spoons, and two wine glasses. Sylvia wondered if Leland would be confused by such elegance, but he wasn't. He seemed to know how to navigate the intricacies of a formal dinner, even how to use the finger bowl.

After dinner they moved into the library for coffee and liqueurs. Conversation flowed and about nine o'clock Melanie and Leland left.

"What do you think," Sylvia asked Lawrence.

"I was impressed. Of course Melanie tutored him on how to behave at the dinner table."

"I thought the same thing," Sylvia said and nodded.

"But most men would have resisted the coaching, thinking it was all too hoity-toity. But not Leland. It showed me he clearly loves her and you could tell she adores him. She kept staring at him."

"Do you think he's a fortune hunter?"

"Absolutely not. He has too much pride, but I do think he loves Melanie because she has class and that's one of the things he likes about her. He's also got success written all over him. Melanie should snap him up before someone else does."

Sylvia seemed thoughtful. "I tend to agree with you, but he hasn't proposed."

"He will. Just give him time and stay out of the picture. But be supportive and tell Melanie what a nice young man he is."

The next day Melanie called and told Sylvia how much Leland enjoyed meeting her and Lawrence. Sylvia told her how much she approved of him.

That afternoon the telephone rang and an angry unfamiliar voice greeted Sylvia. "Hello, my name is Merrill Musgrove. Am I speaking with Sylvia Hutchins?"

"You are," she replied.

The accent was Southern. She guessed it was Leland's father.

"Well, my son told me last night he was interested in marrying your daughter. I must tell you Leland is my only child and my pride and joy. So I asked around about your daughter and found out she's not exactly who she says she is. By that I mean she had a series of drug-related arrests. I haven't discussed this with Leland, but I think you and I should meet and talk this thing over."

Sylvia was so shocked by these comments she wasn't sure what to do. So she agreed to meet Merrill that evening at his home in Riviera Beach. The house was as she suspected, a modest tract home in an older section of Riviera Beach. The door was opened by a man who was slim with an erect bearing and a pencil mustache. He certainly was military, Sylvia thought.

He invited her into the living room and offered her a cup of coffee. Military photos covered the walls and a Japanese Samurai sword hung over the large television set. He returned with two cups of coffee and sat down on his green Barcalounger.

He told Sylvia about his military experience and how he had hoped his son would follow him. Then his expression seemed to change and he seemed wistful, Sylvia thought.

"I'm a widower. My wife died ten years ago and I've raised Leland by myself. I don't have to tell you, because you've met him, how extremely proud I am of him and I want to make sure his life is a happy one."

Sylvia interrupted. "I'm also alone. My husband died five years ago and I feel the same way about Melanie as you do about Leland."

Merrill stood up and walked back into the kitchen to refill the coffee cups. Returning to the living room, he sat down on his Barcalounger and leaned forward, staring directly into Sylvia's eyes. "Let's put our cards on the table, Mrs. Hutchins."

"Please call me Sylvia," she said.

"Okay, Sylvia. I have friends in the police department and also at the hospital. They told me some bad things about your daughter."

Sylvia gritted her teeth. "My daughter has always had a weight problem and when she was a teenager she started taking pep pills to lose weight." Sylvia bit her lip to fight back tears. "These were pills prescribed by a doctor who was highly recommended, but she became addicted to them." Sylvia started to sob. "I blame myself for her difficulties. I guess you know she was arrested for buying what they call Reds and then she had a nervous breakdown. It's all my fault," Sylvia said and sobbed more. "She's really a nice girl and I know she loves your son and would make him a fine wife."

Merrill placed his hand over Sylvia's. "I know how you must feel. My son has been a large part of my life since his mother died. He's a good boy. I know he'll be a fine husband and a good provider."

Sylvia wiped her eyes and looked at Merrill. "He told me he wants to open his own men's store. You know I can help him get started," she said in a wary tone.

Merrill stiffened. "We don't want your money, Sylvia. My son can do it on his own, but thanks anyway. You know, after meeting you and hearing your story, I think I'm changing my mind. I'm not going to mention this meeting to Leland or what I know about Melanie. Let the young people work it out themselves."

He stood up and walked Sylvia to the front door. "It's been very nice meeting you and I hope I'll see you again."

Sylvia leaned forward and kissed him gently on the lips. "I'm sure you will," she replied.

PENANCE

Oliver Farnsworth awoke with a start and sat up in bed. His tee shirt was soaked and perspiration dripped from his hair. A dream - thank God it wasn't the usual dream, the one he'd had over and over for the last thirty-five years. In that dream he was back in college on his way to class, but he didn't have the textbook and didn't know what the course was about. Outside the classroom other students asked where he'd been - he'd missed so many classes. "He'd just been too busy," he replied in an offhand manner.

"There's going to be a midterm test today," one of the students said. Oliver asked to look at his text, but when the student handed it to him there was no writing on the cover and when he opened the book all the pages were blank.

Oliver felt this dream meant he wasn't prepared for life's demands, but he had just awakened from a different dream which was even scarier. He was taking a test in a classroom, but he knew none of the answers. He asked, really demanded, the student sitting in front of him give him his answer sheet. When he handed it to him, Oliver looked at it. The answers confused him. They were all unfamiliar, complicated equations. He heard the exam proctor approach and threw the paper on the floor under his desk. When the proctor passed he looked down and now the floor was covered with test papers. He rifled through them, but couldn't find the one he was looking for. This search seemed to last a long time and he felt tired from the exertion. Then the bell rang, the class ended, and he walked out without turning in his test paper.

This dream was even eerier than the usual one because he felt it meant that he was not only overwhelmed by life, but there was no one who could help him. He would have to solve his problems without assistance. These difficulties weren't that serious he tried to tell himself, but they had to be addressed soon.

Oliver, a widower, now lived in Palm Beach so he could be near his only living relative, his sister. A retired Professor of Romance Languages, he had last taught at the University of Florida in Gainesville. There he owned a condominium which he had bought for $250,000 in 2006 at the height of the real estate boom, but its current value had dropped almost thirty-five percent. So when he moved to Palm Beach he decided to rent it instead of selling it. The condo management team took care of everything and he was happy to cash the monthly check and pay them a five percent management fee.

But they were suddenly unable to rent it and the apartment was vacant. Months passed and finally he received a call from Barry, the on-site realtor. He told Oliver that he had an offer for $225,000, but he seemed too eager and Oliver was suspicious. At first he accepted the offer and then changed his mind. The realtor tried to convince him that this was a good offer and he should sell, but Oliver remained adamant.

He then called his former academic assistant who still lived in Gainesville and asked her to recommend a realtor. She gave him the name of Karen Stoller and told Oliver she was very helpful with a kind and sweet personality. Oliver called her and she accepted the listing, but after a month there was no activity. Finally she called him and asked if he would sell the unit without selling the attached garage. He agreed and she emailed him a "Parcel Cutout" request from the Alachua County Property Appraiser's Office. The office would assign different tax numbers to the condo and to the garage. It was Friday afternoon and Oliver prepared for the weekend, but he filled out the form, drove to the UPS office in West Palm Beach and faxed it.

He felt the condo would be easier to sell. A buyer could own it without the garage for $225,000 and someone else who lived in the complex could own the garage for $25,000. It was early in May, a good time to sell.

He didn't hear from Karen for over a week and assumed she was busy selling his condo until he received an email asking when he was going to send in the "Parcel Cutout." Oliver read the email in disbelief. He had sent it in a week ago and had gotten a fax confirming it had been received. He called Karen immediately and told her he had sent in the form. She replied that it was not showing up on her computer.

"Why didn't you call the Property Appraiser's Office," he asked in an aggressive manner.

"I didn't think I had to."

"Oh, come on," he shouted. "This is ridiculous. I thought by now the condo would be sold. Now you've asked if I've sent the form in."

"Are you sure it was received?"

Anger boiled up in his mouth and he shouted, "Of course I'm sure it was received. I have a receipt."

"Look, I'm sorry, Mr. Farnsworth. I'm not used to being spoken to in this manner. If you want to cancel the listing, that's fine with me."

"No, no, no. You come highly recommended. I'm just very disappointed. Alright. Let's not talk anymore." He said good-bye. He immediately emailed her and apologized for his outburst, but expressed his extreme disappointment and hoped she would straighten it out with the Appraiser's Office and sell the condo.

Now he didn't know what to do. To complicate matters, he received an email from an unknown person telling him he could rent his unit for $1,500 per weekend during the football season when the University of Florida played at home. This would be about $10,500 instead of the $20,400 if he rented it annually. Well, it was an option, but one that didn't appeal. He imagined a lot of noise, complaining neighbors, broken glasses, and stained carpets. Of course the rest of the year he could stay in his condo if he wanted to, but he didn't.

Oliver waited a week and then emailed Karen. He was still angry with her and didn't wish to talk on the phone. He told her he was driving to Gainesville and could they meet on Friday at 3:00 p.m. at the condominium complex. She returned his email and they agreed on the time. At the bottom she wrote that the management of the condo wanted to know if he wished to rent his condo. This complicated the situation even more. He had never met Sarah, the woman who handled renters, but he'd had heated telephone conversations with her about her inability to find a renter.

Oliver's head began to throb. He would go to the condo around 2:00 p.m. on Friday when presumably Brian, the on-site realtor, and Sarah had returned from lunch. He knew he would have to be both charming and forceful and alert to all possibilities.

He walked in the office at exactly 2:00 and saw a young woman sitting at the assistant's desk. "You must be Sarah," he said and smiled. "I'm Oliver Farnsworth, the guy who has been torturing you about renting my condo." He shook hands and stared intently into her blue eyes. She looked like a college student, perhaps a graduate student. "I want to apologize. I guess I was rude."

"Not at all," she said. "I've got good news. I've got three people who want to rent your place."

"Great. Call them up right away."

"But it's listed for sale, isn't it?"

"It is, but it won't be for long. Is Barry in?"

She pointed to the adjoining office. Oliver walked in and shut the door. Barry gave him a quizzical look.

"Okay, okay. I'm a son of a bitch and not a gentleman. What can I tell you? I just thought the offer was not good enough."

Barry's eyes narrowed. "You should have taken it. Now they've already bought something else."

"Look, I'm sorry about the whole mess, but I'm going to fire Karen, the realtor who has the listing, and give it back to you."

Barry looked surprised and gave Oliver a sly look. "She has to agree to the cancellation of the listing."

"She will, she will. I promise you." Oliver felt his adrenaline pumping. Anything was now possible. "You'll get the listing, but you'll have to sell it while it's rented."

"It will be harder to sell, but it's doable."

"Okay. I'm meeting the realtor in twenty minutes. Are you going to be around later?"

Barry nodded.

Oliver was supposed to meet Karen at 3:00 p.m. in the condo clubhouse. At 3:15 his cellphone rang and Karen told him she was at his unit waiting for him. He walked up the small hill and he saw her wave to him. From a distance he could see she was a large overweight woman with thick horn-rimmed glasses, dyed blond hair with black roots showing. She was dressed in an ill-fitting, nondescript pants suit. She looked like she sounded on the phone - tentative, unsure, somewhat needy. She opened the lockbox and they toured his condo. He hadn't seen it in five years, but it brought back no memories, positive or negative. It looked clean and neat, he felt, and would be an easy sale.

They stopped in the kitchen and Oliver turned to her and spoke in a quiet tone. "You know, I must tell you, Karen. I'm very disappointed in your efforts to sell this place. You said you'd cancel the listing if I wished to and I'd like to."

She opened her folder and took out a single sheet of paper. "Everyone else appreciates my efforts, even if you don't." Her voice was shaky. "I've already made out the cancellation agreement. You can sign it and I'll send you a copy."

"No, no. We can go to the clubhouse now and make copies there."

She agreed. He walked briskly back to the clubhouse. Karen followed in her car.

"I've done it," he shouted as he walked in the office. Barry seemed surprised.

"Make out a management agreement," he said to Sarah. Karen walked in the office. Oliver doubted she'd heard the conversation.

"I'm sorry I won't see you again," Sarah said. It was a pleasure doing business with you." A tear came to her eyes and her speech faltered.

Oliver felt he should be pleased. In less than an hour his condo was rented, one realtor fired and another previously fired was now rehired. What an accomplishment, but he felt somehow sad. He was the good guy, wasn't he? When he played tennis he always wore white clothes and a white hat. At least he thought he was the good guy.

This was business, he reminded himself, and sometimes you had to be a bastard, but he still felt bad. Karen was sweet, kind and helpful, traits that meant something. Oliver had spent too much time in Academe where reputation and tenure were what mattered and in Palm Beach which was all about looks and show. He had become an elitist and was out of touch with real people, real values, and he knew it.

He fumbled for his glasses in his pocket, but they weren't there. He asked if anyone had seen them. It didn't really matter. They were reading glasses he'd bought at a Dollar Store.

"There's a Walmart down the street," Sarah said. "Why don't you go there?"

As he walked from the parking lot to Walmart a street person approached him. He was dirty and unshaven. His teeth were black and chipped and he had an unpleasant body odor. Oliver couldn't tell if he was a wino or a wacko.

"Hey, buddy. Could you spare a dollar for a cup of coffee?"

"Sure. Why not," Oliver replied. He reached in his pocket, pulled out his wallet and withdrew a dollar. Then he put it back and took out a twenty.

"Buy yourself twenty cups of coffee," he said to the man and handed him the bill. He continued to walk toward the store. He noticed the man followed him.

"Oh, thank you, sir. Thank you. May God bless you, sir. You're very kind."

EMPTY NESTER

Daphne de Rham had made a smooth transition - that's what she called it and indeed it was. She had gone from stay-at-home soccer mom, president of the Garden Club, chairman of the Heart Ball Committee to being a successful entrepreneur.

It had been much easier than she thought possible, but there were problems. Her husband Charlie, a Palm Beach dermatologist, was jealous. An old-fashioned kind of guy, he thought the husband should be the breadwinner while the little woman stayed at home in the background. Charlie was not only a doctor but something of a Palm Beach legend. He had rowed stroke on the Yale Heavyweight Crew the year they won The Race, Henley and the Olympics. At six-feet-five he was an imposing figure and all Palm Beach knew about his exploits. Bald with a shaved head when Daphne met him, she thought he looked like Daddy Warbucks.

His practice originally flourished, but lately some of his patients had left him. They complained he was too eager to do Mohs surgery when calcium chloride would suffice.

Dermatologists were usually very busy in Florida. Sun damage was rampant and appointments were difficult to make. However, these doctors were resented. Up north only teenagers with acne problems went to dermatologists. In Palm Beach everyone seemed to be a patient. A tiny spot on one's face needed surgery it seemed. How could one argue with the doctor? If you disagreed, the only option was another dermatologist.

Daphne's new career was really a godsend with Bart at Williams, Amanda at Choate, and Will at Cornell. The de Rham household was stretched for cash.

Charlie had taken a second mortgage on their home, but it wasn't enough. Tuition fees of $150,000 per year were a drain.

Daphne's new career as an interior designer was what the de Rham household needed, but her business had grown so fast that now she needed help. She had begun by working out of her home. A former Ford fashion model, she had always been a Palm Beach style leader. Her home, which she was constantly remodeling, was the envy of her friends. When some of them asked if she would redecorate their homes, Daphne was delighted to help. She had business cards printed up that read "Daphne de Rham, Interior Designs." Underneath the phrase was "The Palm Beach Look."

The Palm Beach Look was basically an old money look with a lighter palette. Daphne made heavy use of the citrus colors - orange, yellow and lime - plus complementary tones like pink, mauve and aubergine. Lighter colors used with traditional English and French furniture, which had been vermeiled, created a look that was brighter and cleaner. Daphne also had a keen sense of spatial relations - where to place furniture, paintings, knickknacks. Everyone said her homes were glamorous and exciting, but also warm and inviting.

She had studied the works of the classic designers: Billy Baldwin, Nancy Lancaster, Albert Hadley, John Fowler, Elsie de Wolfe, Eleanor McMillen, Mario Buatta and the designer she felt a kinship with, Sister Parish. Like Sister, Daphne was basically untrained and self-taught, but she admired good design and had a sensitive appreciation for all things beautiful.

Following in the steps of Sister Parish, she now felt she needed an associate, a man who had studied and one who held an American Society of Interior Designers card. A friend told her about Oscar Van Alstyne who had retired to Palm Beach after working in New York for McMillen. Daphne agreed to meet him for tea at her home. The silver service was set on the coffee table when he walked in.

"Hi, I'm Oscar Van Alstyne," he said.

Daphne stood up and greeted him warmly. She was impressed by his appearance. A full head of wavy salt and pepper hair, prominent Roman nose, strong jawline and light brown eyes. Dressed in a subtle pinstriped blue suit with a light blue shirt and a small patterned red tie with a matching pocket square, he exuded good taste.

"A pleasure to meet you," she said and smiled. "I can tell at a glance you're the right person for the job. However, I must tell you that my husband is an extremely jealous man. So I must know if you are gay."

Oscar looked surprised. "You don't waste words, do you? Yes, I am gay and proud of it."

"Good, excellent as a matter of fact. I plan to open a small showroom on the Via Parigi off of Worth Avenue. I'm well known in Palm Beach and business is excellent - too good, really. I need help and I think you can provide it."

They agreed on terms, decided to rent a small space on the Via Parigi, and opened for business. The showroom was really a living room decorated in the Palm Beach style.

A lot of passersby walked in, which led to even more business, but life at home had begun to deteriorate. Charlie kept nagging Daphne about being too "ballsy." He wondered what had happened to that sweet debutante he married. Daphne explained the pressure of business had made her more aggressive and commanding, but Charlie was still displeased. He reminded her they had a second mortgage on their home which more than covered their children's education. What he didn't remind her about was that his practice was faltering and they really did need the money she was bringing in.

When Daphne told Charlie she had hired an assistant who was a man, he was furious and demanded to meet him. Daphne tried to reassure him that Oscar was gay, but Charlie insisted on meeting him. Charlie stopped by her shop one day during lunch hour and watched through the window as they examined a book of fabrics. They were sitting very close to each other and Charlie started to fume before he walked in.

Surprised by his appearance, Daphne quickly introduced Oscar who stood up and shook hands. Charlie's peevishness was obvious and after a perfunctory look around he said, "It all looks very nice, but I have to get back to work."

"Very rude, I would say. What's wrong with that man?"

"I told you he's very jealous."

"But I'm gay. You must have told him."

"Of course I did, but you don't look it or act it and now he's not going to believe me." Daphne slammed the fabric book shut. "This business has created a huge strain on our marriage but I don't care. I'm not going to give it up. I finally am beginning to express myself and enjoy my life and Charlie's not going to rain on my parade." She looked over at Oscar. "I'm finally owning up to the fact, after twenty-five years, Charlie and I are not well suited to each other.

He's a real outdoorsy type who likes to hunt and fish and go airboat riding in the Everglades - things that I detest." Her expression became rueful. "I should have married someone like you. Too bad you're gay. We like the same things - fashion, style, art, theater, symphony, opera. We would be companionable and have plenty to talk about."

Oscar reached over and clasped her hands. "We can still do all these things together."

Daphne shook her head. "I don't think so. I don't see myself getting a divorce. I've got three great children that I'm very proud of. They are in school now and need my help."

"That reminds me. I was going to ask you. Why don't you have your daughter come in and lend a hand. She doesn't have to know much, you know, no pun intended. Just sort of decorate the place."

Daphne slumped in her chair. "Amanda is a very nice girl, but she takes after her father. She's big and strong an raw boned and when she graduates from Choate she wants to join the Army and go to Afghanistan."

Oscar looked shocked.

"No, she doesn't take after her mother."

"No, I guess not. Wow," he looked thoughtful. "She's smart. She doesn't want to compete with you. So she's gone in a different direction. My sister tried to follow in my mother's footsteps, but she didn't have the right stuff and it just never worked out."

The door of the shop opened and a well-dressed middle-aged woman walked in. She introduced herself and started to look around. "I love it. I love the look. I'm visiting in Palm Beach, but I have a home in Southhampton which I'd like you to decorate. You know, you should open a shop on Job's Lane. I'm sure you'd do well in the Hamptons."

Daphne and Oscar stared at each other. Two days previous a woman had walked in and suggested they open a shop in Newport.

"Well, we're very busy right now, but perhaps in the future we might be able to help you."

"Well, if you ever think of opening in Southhampton, give me a call," she said and handed Daphne her card. "I'm in real estate. Perhaps I can find a spot for you."

After the woman left Oscar hugged Daphne. "This is great. I know someone in New York who can open the place in Southhampton and I have a buddy who is retired and living in Newport who can open the shop there."

Daphne looked at him askance. "Do you really think we can make a go of it in all three locations?"

"Yes, of course. It means a lot of travel and being away from home a lot."

"Charlie is going to love this. Well, he's going to have to like it. I will talk to him this evening."

That evening Daphne sat in her living room sipping a mojito and glancing at the Shiny Sheet. It was cocktail hour, but Charlie was late. Finally at the stroke of six Charlie walked in and went right to the drinks table and mixed himself a Beefeater Martini. Sitting in one of the chairs in front of the couch he glared at Daphne. Slowly she folded her paper and took a sip from her drink.

"I must tell you I was very upset today when I visited your shop."

"Oh, really? Why?" Daphne feigned innocence. She was going to try to keep this conversation civilized.

"You seemed to be too cozy with your assistant or your associate or whatever he calls himself."

"Oh, Oscar? Well, he's harmless. I told you he was gay."

"Well, he sure didn't look like it or seem like it." Charlie gulped his drink.

"Well, that's good. I'm glad you said that. It'll be good for business."

Daphne could tell Charlie was seething, but he couldn't find the right words.

"Look, Daphne, I don't like this interior design," he stammered, "thing. You've changed. You're not the woman I married. You've become bossy and aggressive and I don't like it." He slammed his glass on the table. "Let me remind you again. I've taken a second mortgage on the house. So the tuition for the kids is covered. I don't know why you have to go into business."

Daphne sipped her drink slowly. "Well, I think you'll agree it's nice to have the extra cash."

"But we don't need it. I'm the breadwinner in this household and we have enough," he thundered.

"Darling, I know you're the breadwinner and you've always been a good provider." She was stroking him. She didn't mention how his practice had faltered and they had to cut back on extravagances. "But you want me to be happy, don't you? You know I'm an empty nester and this gives me something to do."

"What about your club work and charity work?"

"I've done all that. It's time to move on." Daphne began to resent this conversation. "Look, Charlie, we have an opportunity to expand the business and open up branches in Southhampton and Newport and we're going to do it."

Charlie stood up and threw his glass into the fireplace. "This is ridiculous. Why did I ever marry you," he said and stormed out of the room.

Daphne put her drink down, removed her iPhone from her bag and dialed. "I'd like to make a first class reservation for two on your first flight tomorrow morning to Islip Airport on Long Island," she said. "And have a car and driver waiting to take us to Southhampton."

LOTTERY LOSER

Homer Watson should have been a happy man. He had won the Iowa Lottery in 2006, retired and moved from Des Moines to Palm Beach. He had $50 million to spend and he was determined to enjoy his money.

Formerly an accountant in the Mercy Medical Center, he knew numbers and considered himself a sensible man. He understood money couldn't buy happiness, but it could beguile the hours and ease the pain of the loss of his beloved wife Muriel. She had died in a car crash two years before he had won the lottery.

Now a widower with an only son Jeremy he first bought a five-bedroom, five-bath Mizner home, an ocean-going yacht and a vintage Rolls-Royce. When he moved he inquired about joining some of the Palm Beach clubs. He was told he had to have a proposal letter and three seconding letters. Since he knew no one in Palm Beach this was impossible. So he played golf and tennis at the public facilities.

He asked about working on one of the charities and he was accepted immediately. When he met with the committee and told them he was a widower they eagerly introduced him to unmarried committee members. Between golf and tennis and charity work, Homer made lots of new friends and led a full and busy life.

However, Homer was concerned that maybe his luxurious lifestyle had made his son spoiled and unmotivated. Basically a good boy, he had a passion for fast cars and had acquired many speeding tickets.

His son had just graduated from Northwestern and was now set to go out into the world. They met on Homer's Yacht the ARGO to discuss his future. The sun was setting and they sat on the fantail sipping wine. It was a beautiful late afternoon with the sun gently shining on the water.

"Look, Jeremy, I'm not in the advice business. I've told you before you've got to figure it all out for yourself. I can't help you."

"But, Dad, I'm coming to you because I need your help."

Jeremy seemed so needy, so lost, Homer thought. "Sorry, son. I've given you two pieces of advice. One, don't marry until you're thirty and, two, manage your own money. The rest is up to you. Look, I've told you all this before. My father used to drive me crazy with his advice. He'd start every sentence with, 'If you want the benefit of my experience,' and I'd want to say, 'No, I don't - I want to experience it myself,' but I was too respectful. Then he'd say, 'If I were you,' and that really got to me and I'd want to scream, 'You're not me.' So remember, if anybody ever says to you, 'If I were you,' they are telling you what they would do. Best to ignore their advice."

Jeremy started to shake his head. I don't know what to do. I've got my Bachelor's Degree in History from Northwestern, but I'm not interested in teaching history and that's about the only thing it's good for."

"Why don't you get an advanced degree. Then you can write books about history."

"I'm not interested. I kind of wish I'd studied something else, something that would get me a job."

Homer stared at Jeremy. "Look, you can do anything you want and as long as it's legal, I'll be behind you. Selfishly I hope someday not too soon you'll meet a nice girl, settle down and raise a family. I'm looking forward to being a grandfather."

Jeremy sighed. "All this is in the future, Dad. I'm talking about right now."

Homer put down his wine glass. "You know you don't have to do anything. Why don't you travel around the world. Maybe then you'll get some ideas."

"I'm not interested in being a tourist. I want to be actively involved. I want a challenge. I want to do something."

Homer leaned back in his chair. "Well, you know what they say, follow your bliss. What's your bliss?"

"I don't know. That's why we're talking. I know that my bliss is not teaching history."

"Can you visualize doing something that interests you, anything?"

"You mean like having sex with Cindy?" They both laughed.

"No, I don't mean that. I mean something worthwhile that you can earn a living doing. Alright, let's try a different approach," Homer said exasperated. "Describe to me your perfect day. Tell me what you would do from morn to night."

Jeremy looked up at the setting sun. "Well, the first thing I'd do is to take my Lambo for a spin on the Turnpike. Then

I guess I'd go home and have breakfast - fruit cup, western omelet, French fries. Then I'd call Cindy, you know, my girlfriend, and set up a lunch date at the Breakers or the Colony and invite some friends. Then I guess it would be matinee time after lunch, laying pipe as they say. Then we might take a run up to Disney World in the Lambo, have dinner at the French Pavilion, and then drive back to Palm Beach.

Homer had given Jeremy a Lamborghini Huracan as a graduation present. He told Jeremy he could have any car that he desired, but he thought he might choose a Corvette or Shelby Ford.

"Hmmm, well, that's kind of interesting. So selfish pleasure is your guiding principle." Homer noticed Jeremy looking away. So he raised his hand. "Look, I didn't expect you to do charity work, read a book, visit a museum, watch the sun set or visit me. Okay. You're trying to find yourself, but you don't have to find yourself today, tomorrow or even next year. Take your time. You're probably going to live to be ninety and maybe you'll reinvent yourself a couple of times."

Jeremy looked plaintive. "So what should I do right now, Dad?"

"You mentioned the Lamborghini. In fact, aside from Cindy that's the only thing you mentioned twice. I hesitate to say this because you're my only child and I love you very much, but have you ever thought about becoming a Formula One race driver?"

Jeremy looked up and his eyes brightened. "No, Dad, I haven't, but that's a great idea. I've always liked cars and even when I was younger I liked to tinker with them.

I know what goes on under the hood and that helps if you want to be a driver."

Homer bit his lip. He wished he hadn't mentioned auto racing. His wife Muriel had died in an auto wreck twelve years previous and he'd never fully recovered from the shock.

"How would I go about it, becoming a Formula One driver?"

"I haven't a clue," Homer said and tears formed in his eyes. Homer knew boys from Jeremy's privileged background liked fast cars and many had died in accidents. Maybe we should have stayed in Des Moines, he thought. No, he had to get away and forget about Muriel's death. That's what he'd spent his money doing, trying to forget about the only woman he'd ever loved.

Ten years later Jeremy had achieved his goal and was now one of the top Formula One drivers in the world. He made over $40 million per year, not that he needed the money. He owned four homes in three continents, beautiful women fought to be close to him, but he still hadn't married and Homer wondered whether he'd ever be a grandfather.

One night Homer awoke with a stabbing pain in his side. He arose and started to pace. It's happened. Homer felt it. His son had died in a car crash. He fell back into bed and sobbed. He died doing what he loved. "I guess a man has to do what he has to do," he said aloud.

TWO DIFFERENT WORLDS

It was an unusual way to meet, Mark Dore remembered. He was walking up the Spanish Steps and she was walking down. He stopped and stared when she was a few steps above him, "Haven't I seen you someplace before," he asked.

"Oh, come on. Can't you do better than that? This is Rome, remember, and I get hit on at least five times a day."

"I'm not surprised. You really are beautiful."

She was, he thought. Blond hair, high cheekbones, eyes as blue as the Roman sky, teeth so bright he thought they shone like diamonds.

"'Worn out phrases and longing gazes.' You know the song," she said and walked past him. The competition is ferocious here in Rome. You've got to come up with a better line than that.

He followed her like a puppy dog. "But I really mean it. I honestly think I've seen you before."

She stopped, turned and stared at him. "And where might that have been," she said in an imperious tone.

"In Palm Beach. That's where I live."

"Me, too, but I don't think we travel in the same circles."

This was a not too subtle put-down, but Mark persisted. "I think we do," he said and smiled. "I'm sure I remember seeing you at an art opening at the Wally Findlay Gallery."

"You might have, you just might have." She continued to walk. "Look, I appreciate your compliments. I really do, but I'm on my way to do some shopping on the Via Condotti."

"Do you mind if I join you?"

"You certainly are persistent," she replied and increased her pace. "I must tell you I'm engaged. You know, engaged to be married and am here for a brief trip. So I really see no point in continuing this conversation."

"What about a cup of coffee at Caffe Greco?"

"Why are you so determined," she snapped.

"Well, I live in Palm Beach and, I don't know, maybe we know some of the same people and anyway it's hot, your feet must be sore - mine are - and would it hurt to have a cup of coffee with a fellow American and fellow Palm Beacher?"

She sighed and looked at her watch. "Well, I certainly commend your persistence. My feet are killing me. These flip-flops were a mistake. I guess a cup of coffee isn't such a bad idea. At least you're not like these Italian men - all hands and flowery phrases. It gets old, believe me."

The caffe was crowded with tourists but they found a table and sat side by side on a deep red velvet banquette. A waiter in a tail coat and a wing collar brought them their order of two espressos.

"I think Worth Avenue needs a place like this. It's really charming. By the way, I'm Melinda Graves."

"I'm Mark Dore." He extended his hand and she put hers out. He shook it and wouldn't let go.

"Come on, Mark. You're American, remember? Stop acting like these Italian men. You know, I must have passed this place twenty times, but I've never been in here."

"It's great, isn't it," Mark said looking around. "High ceilings, classic paintings on the walls, good food. You know it's Rome's oldest restaurant. It opened in 1760 and a lot of famous people have dined here. Byron, Keats, Liszt, Wagner, Gogol - even Buffalo Bill. There's a large painting of him in the back."

Melinda stared at Mark. "You say you saw me at Wally Findlay's. Are you interested in art?"

"Well, I appreciate it, but I'm not a real artist. Photography is my hobby. I like to go to the Everglades with my camera and capture the peace and beauty."

"You say it's your hobby. What do you do for a living?"

"I'm a lawyer."

"Do you specialize?"

"Divorce."

"Hah, that's funny. I'll bet you're very busy."

"Yes, I am. I hope you'll never be a client."

They both laughed.

"I couldn't help noticing that rock on your left hand. It must be your engagement ring."

Melinda twisted it on her finger. "Six carats. It's nice, isn't it?"

"Your fiance must be loaded."

"He is. Brian's family is originally from Indianapolis. They manufactured auto parts - you know, spark plugs, things like that. But that was years ago. They sold the company and Brian is the sole heir."

"So what does he do when he's not counting his money?"

"He's a financial advisor - a stock broker, but that's just his cover. He's really a sportsman."

"Oh? What's his game?"

"Polo is his first sport, but he also competes in golf and tennis. You know, club tournaments."

"Is he interested in art?"

"Not at all." Melinda stroked her chin. "That bothers me for I consider myself an artist. I graduated from Yale with a major in art history and I've studied art here in Rome and in Paris and I still take classes in Palm Beach."

"Are you planning an exhibition at Findlay's?"

"No, no, no." She laughed. "I'm not the next Mary Cassatt. I want to specialize in children's portraits. I love children and like working with pastel chalk. When I was nine an artist who was a deaf mute did my portrait. I'll never forget it - my mother walked in the room where I was sitting and asked the artist for a progress report. He couldn't speak words, but he started grunting and waved my mother out of the room. Needless to say, she was annoyed but she left. You know, Mark, I still look at that portrait. He really captured me and someday I hope to be able to do work like he did."

"Wow, you really get excited when you talk about art and your fiance has no interest?"

"None. Brian's a man's man kind of guy - not that he doesn't like women, which he does, which worries me a bit."

"Do you have a prenuptial agreement?"

"Prenups are passe today. You know that. Anyhow, they don't work. The lawyers drag out the cases and they end up getting all the money. But the subject came up recently. At Brian's suggestion when we get married he's going to place a million dollars in a checking account in my name."

"Wow, this sounds like a business agreement, not a marriage. Do you really love this guy and does he love you?"

"Look, Mark, you know better than I do, marriage is a very iffy business. I've got to protect myself. These sportsmen like to party and there are always these groupies hanging around." Melinda stopped talking and looked at Mark. "I don't know why I'm telling you all this. Let's talk about you. For starters, where's your camera?"

"I left it in the hotel room, but I've got my iPhone." He removed it from his pocket and snapped a picture of Melinda and looked at it. "Not bad. You really are beautiful."

He stopped a waiter and asked him to take a picture of the two of them. He moved next to her and put his cheek against hers. He noticed the softness of her skin and she was wearing his favorite scent, La Vie Est Belle. He looked at the photo the waiter had taken and shook his head. "Gosh, it looks like Beauty and the Beast." The contrast was extreme, he thought, with his dark hair, oyster complexion, brown eyes which were too close together and eyebrows which formed one continuous line.

"I don't think so," Melinda said. "You're the dark stranger. I think you look intriguing." She gazed around the room and then at her espresso cup. It had an orange and black stripe and Caffe Greco, A.D. 1760 was engraved on it. "Everything is so beautiful here, even this cup." She raised it to her lips and finished her coffee. "Well, I'm going to the loo and then I must do some shopping."

When she left Mark went to the cashier's desk and priced the espresso cup and saucer. It was almost $150. Oh, why not, he thought. The grand gesture. Maybe next time she'll remember me.

When she came back they walked out of the restaurant together. He took his hand from behind his back and handed her the package. "A little remembrance," he said.

She stepped back. "What is it?"

"An espresso cup with the Caffe Greco logo."

She handed the box back to him. "I can't accept gifts from strangers."

He shrugged and smiled. I don't consider us strangers. After all, this is the second time we've met.

She looked at him and grinned. "It's a very nice gesture, but I'm going to pass. But if we ever meet again I'm sure I'll remember you."

"Here's my business card," he said and handed it to her. He took her other hand, bowed low, and kissed it. "Arrivederci, signorina." He waved to her as she strolled down the Via Condotti.

Three weeks later the phone rang in Mark's office. "It's Melinda. You'll be happy to hear I returned the engagement ring."

"Glad to hear it," Mark replied. "The Findlay Gallery is having an art opening this evening. Could we meet there?"

There was a pause on the other end. "Only if you promise not to use that tired old line, 'Haven't I seen you someplace before?'"

RAILROAD RAPPROCHEMENT

It was September 12, 2001 and Curry Fitzhugh wanted out of New York. He wanted to get back to Palm Beach, but couldn't. The planes were grounded. He didn't want to rent a car and drive back. The trains, he thought, must still run. He called Amtrak but the phone lines were jammed.

He left his mother's apartment at 63rd and 5th and walked to Penn Station. It was a grim experience. Smoke hung over the city like a pall and the smell of dead bodies started to waft uptown. The streets were crowded with walkers, but at the direction of the Mayor they were all headed uptown while Curry was going downtown. Their faces were haggard and their eyes darted about, probably wondering who was the next terrorist. Everyone looked up at a noise in the sky, but it was only the sound of military jets guarding against the next attack.

Curry had begged his mother to leave and join him, but like Stalin in Moscow, when the Nazis were at the gates, she refused to leave New York. When he stood in the ticket line and looked around everyone seemed anxious or scared or both. The ticket sellers were overwhelmed by the crush of customers, but he was lucky and booked a Viewliner Bedroom on the Silver Meteor leaving at 3:15 p.m. the next day and arriving in Palm Beach at 4:54 p.m. the following day.

He remembered when he was a small boy taking the same train with his parents to Palm Beach. He had a vague recollection of sleeping in the same bed with his sister, but instead of sleeping side by side he slept with his head at the foot of the bed. He recalled they kicked each other all night long. That was the last time he'd been on a sleeper train, but it was a pleasant experience. He looked forward to the train ride. His fellow passengers would be talkative and he would be able to move around from car to car and there was a diner with smiling stewards. His bedroom had its own bathroom with shower. He was going to enjoy himself.

The train left on time the next day and Curry felt relief just to get out of New York and all the turmoil. Like most New Yorkers, visitors or residents, Curry was shaken by the whole 9/11 experience. He first heard about it on ABC News. Peter Jennings had said there was a report coming in about a jet slamming into the World Trade Center. Then he said maybe we should all sit down, take a deep breath and relax. Jennings didn't believe it could happen. Neither did Curry. His emotions were scrambled. He felt sorrow for the dead and worried there might be another attack.

At dinnertime Curry walked forward to the dining car. It was crowded and he had to sit with three other passengers. Their stories were all similar. They had visited New York on business or pleasure and were eager to return home. This certainly wasn't the 20th Century Limited, Curry thought. No white table cloths, monogrammed silver, crystal stemware and, unlike the movie *North by Northwest*, nobody resembled Cary Grant or Eva Marie Saint.

But someone did look familiar, sitting opposite him on the other side of the dining car. Shannon Cosgrove? Could it be her? It had been almost thirty years since he'd seen her. At that time she was slender, blond and sexy. Now she was red faced, overweight, and blowsy. Her mouth turned down at the corners. Back then he'd loved her and proposed marriage, but she wanted to stay in New York and he wanted to move to Florida. His health had deteriorated, his advertising career had faltered - it was time to make a new start. Shannon worked at a small art gallery as a consultant and wanted to advance her career in New York.

Curry dawdled over his coffee until Shannon left the dining car. He was almost sure she had booked a bedroom. Her clothes looked expensive and she carried an Hermes handbag. He followed her back three cars to the sleeper section and just as she was about to open her bedroom door, he said, "Excuse me. Aren't you Shannon Cosgrove?"

"I am, and you're Curry Fitzhugh," she replied and turned around and appraised him. "Come on in." She closed the sliding door and Velcroed the blue curtains shut. They sat opposite each other and Curry smiled.

"You've changed," he said.

"But you haven't, you lucky bastard. You were always slim and youthful looking. I know I don't look so good anymore, but I've had some hard knocks. Maybe I should have accepted your proposal. After we broke up I met Schuyler Van Siclen."

"You were always impressed by fancy names," he interjected.

Shannon's eyes blazed. "Maybe because you and your snotty family were always putting me down."

"That's not true. Because you came from Montana you were overly sensitive about your hick background."

"But I wasn't a hick. The Cosgroves are one of the first families in Helena."

"Tell me about your career," Curry said changing the subject. "You look like you're doing well."

"I am. I'm a certified art curator and work for a small museum. What about yourself?"

"I changed careers when I moved to Florida. I now work as a trust officer in the West Palm Beach National Bank."

Oh, boy! You finally found your true calling. I'm sure you can relate to all those Palm Beach trust fund babies and remittance men," she said with sarcasm.

"Are you going to Palm Beach now?" He again changed the subject.

"Yes, I have a lot of friends there and one of them was kind enough to invite me down when she heard about 9/11."

"Anyone I might know?"

"I doubt it, unless you belong to the Bath & Tennis or the Everglades Club."

Still insecure, he thought. He was glad he never married her.

"Anyhow, I met this woman - actually another trust officer at the bank. We got married and we now have a teenage daughter."

Shannon's manner softened. "I envy you, Curry. I really do. Schuyler and I moved to the country where he became a gentleman farmer."

"Oh, my God. What possessed you?"

"I thought he loved me and we would get married..."

"Let me finish the story. You spent most of your time drinking and fighting and he decided he didn't want to marry you and you decided you didn't want to live on a farm."

"That's about it, I guess. I should have married you. We sure had some great times."

Curry smiled, "I remember. I remember. We used to smoke pot, turn up the stereo, and make love deep into the night. We listened to the music from *Jesus Christ Superstar* and *Hair*."

Shannon nodded. "Remember *The Horse with No Name*?"

"America," Curry fired back.

"*Taxi*."

"Harry Chapin."

"*Je T'aime*."

"Jane Birkin."

"*Nights in White Satin*."

"The Moody Blues."

"Oh, my God. You do remember those times," Shannon said and smiled.

"Yes, I do. Very clearly. We had some great moments."

All of a sudden Shannon looked sad. "I remember what you said to me once. You said, 'No matter what may happen to either of us, no matter where you may go or what you may say or do, I will always love you.'"

Curry was silent for a moment. "I really said all that?"

"Yes, you did."

"And you remember it? I must have been stoned."

"No, you weren't."

Curry slowly shook his head. "You know, that's the trouble with love. You have all these beautiful feelings, you say all these beautiful things, and you think love is going to last forever, but it never does."

Tears glistened on Shannon's cheeks. "Hold me, Curry. I need a hug."

He sat beside her and put his arms around her. "Maybe, just maybe that's all we have to look forward to - beautiful moments that turn into memories."

Curry could feel his eyes mist over as Shannon started to sob.

NARCISSUS' NEMESIS

Russell Parkhurst brushed his hair while he stared at himself in his bathroom mirror. Each stroke was slow and sensual. He loved the feel of the boar bristles as they flowed through his wavy golden locks and stimulated his scalp. He smiled and admired his shiny white teeth. They lined up in perfect rows and had no fillings.

He dropped his arms by his sides, pushed them inward so his pectoral muscles jumped, then he raised his arms over his head and flexed his biceps. His hard and well formed muscles pleased him.

He blinked and poured Visine drops into his periwinkle blue eyes. Such a delicate, elegant color, he thought. He appraised his small, well formed ears and his full sensuous mouth.

Pursing his lips, he bent forward and kissed the mirror. This ritual he performed every morning and didn't think it odd or unusual.

Russell was happy. He had just turned thirty-five and inherited three million dollars from his father who had died four years earlier. Russell was annoyed the money had been held in trust until he reached thirty-five, but this was not unusual in Palm Beach where parents thought it wiser to withhold inheritances until the heir was mature enough to spend it sensibly. The other half of the trust fund would be paid when Russell reached forty-five. This delayed system of payments was another irritation, but Russell consoled himself by invading the trust for the maximum amount of $20,000 per year.

Now that he had his money, he decided it was time to get married. Russell worked as a Palm Beach realtor, but he rarely made sales and had few listings, but that didn't matter now. What mattered was finding a bride. Because of his good looks he had no trouble with girlfriends, but most of them found him vain and superficial. He found them self-centered fortune hunters and sought women outside of Palm Beach.

One evening he watched the Turner Classic Movie Channel and saw "The Duchess of Idaho," which starred Esther Williams. He had never heard of her, but he was impressed. She seemed so modern. Tall and broad shouldered with long muscular legs, she radiated beauty, health and strength, unlike most of the 1950s divas who were smaller, less well developed and better suited to indoor pleasures.

In her movies Esther was always pursued by her leading man and at least one other rival. She accepted this attention as if it were due her and Russell agreed she deserved it. She had once been an Olympic swimmer hopeful and could also dive off the spring board.

Russell was athletic and considered himself a sportsman. He swam, he sailed, he played golf and tennis. He even tried jai-alai. He was proficient at these sports and won many local tournaments, but he wasn't world class in any of them and it bothered him.

Russell had some idea of marrying an athletic woman like Esther Williams and producing a superstar. He had contacted the editor of the Palm Beach Courant, who was a friend, to writing an article about a diving meet held at The International Swimming Hall of Fame in Fort Lauderdale. The editor said maybe, but that was enough for Russell since he was not writing it for the money. Instead he hoped to meet and possibly date one of the divers.

After breakfast Russell drove to the Bougainvillea Club for his weekly tennis match with Jess Van Sant. Jess taught history at Palm Beach Community College and they had known each other since they were classmates at Palm Beach Day School.

In the locker room Russell told Jess about his idea of marrying an athletic superstar.

"Sounds like you've been reading Mein Kampf," Jess interrupted.

Russell seemed surprised. "That was that book by Hitler, wasn't it? The one he wrote when he was in prison?"

"That's right. It sounds like you're trying, like Hitler, to produce a master race."

"You don't like my idea," Russell replied and frowned.

Jess slammed his locker door. "I think it's ridiculous. What's wrong with Palm Beach women?"

Russell pondered the question. "I don't know. They just don't appeal to me. Too self-centered and too egotistical."

"And you're not? Oh, come on, Russ. You're living in a fantasy world. You're going to meet this woman, this diver, who is going to produce these world class athletes - someone who has probably never heard of Palm Beach, someone you have nothing in common with ..."

"Look, most of the women I know are gold diggers."

Jess sighed and lifted his eyebrows. "Palm Beach is all about money. If you can't handle that idea, you don't belong here."

"I know it's all about money," Russell replied, raising his voice, "but I find it offensive. That's all anyone thinks about and talks about."

"Okay. So you want to meet this superstar who is naive and probably not too bright so you can dominate and manipulate her."

"Russ," Jess said placing his hands on Russell's shoulders, "you're clearly a narcissist."

"What's this narcissism shit about? That's all I hear these days. Until recently I never heard the word mentioned."

"Somebody wrote a book on the subject and you're right, it seems to be a popular topic of conversation and, Russ old buddy, you fit the bill."

"What do you mean," Russell replied and placed his hands on his hips in a defiant pose.

"Well, just to name a few characteristics: grandiosity in ideas, sense of self-importance, preoccupied with fantasies of unlimited success, strong sense of entitlement, arrogant behavior or attitudes - sound like anybody we know?" Jess spoke sarcastically.

"Thanks a lot. I thought you were my friend."

"I am your friend. Can't you see I'm trying to help you?"

Russell shook his head. "Hmm, I don't know. Let's play tennis."

Russell lost 6-1, 6-1. Usually the matches were close, but he was so distracted by Jess' comments that he couldn't concentrate. He admitted to himself that he was a narcissist, but so what? Was that so terrible? Now he felt even more determined to seek his dream.

It was a gorgeous day in early May. The sky a radiant blue and a sweet breeze blew off the ocean which was across the street from The International Swimming Hall of Fame. The meet was in progress when Russell arrived. There were only about fifty spectators in the small grandstand. He heard the judges' scores as he approached the grandstand: "Six, six and one-half, five, five and one-half." It was all familiar to him from watching Olympic Games diving on television. He opened his program and learned this was a Grand Prix event that attracted sixty-five divers from fifteen countries and they all hoped to qualify for the 2016 Olympic Games in Rio De Janeiro.

Platform diving seemed like a lot of fun, Russell thought. Soaring, spinning, twisting, whirling into the sky, then plunging like a pelican into the sapphire water. He flipped the pages of his program and learned more about the divers and the competition.

Suddenly the crowd screamed. He looked up from his program to see a diver falling limply into the water, blood streaming from his head.

"Get him. Get him," an official yelled.

Immediately three divers jumped in and pulled him out of the water. Maybe this isn't so much fun, Russell thought. Hitting one's head on the platform must be a constant fear. They carried the unconscious diver into the locker room and after a brief intermission the competition continued. None of the divers seemed upset by the accident.

The men's event ended and the women's platform diving began. Russell thought about his conversation with Jess - how he thought Russell was interested in a naive woman he could manipulate and dominate. He doubted he could dominate any of these divers. They were obviously extremely brave with strong personalities.

After the women's event ended, many of the competitors joined the small crowd on the grandstand to watch the men's three meter. The woman who came in second sat near Russell. He had seen her walk over towards the grandstand and he liked her. She walked with erect posture, held her head high, and had an athletic femininity which reminded him of Esther Williams.

"Hi," he said and smiled broadly. She blinked and backed away slightly. He was overdoing it, he realized. Too manic. He had to tone it down.

"Hi," she smiled back at him.

"Wow, that was some performance. Sorry you didn't win, but second place isn't too shabby."

She grimaced and shook her head. "I messed up that triple somersault and it cost me first place."

Russell eyed her intently. Tall with broad shoulders and small breasts, she had magnificent coloring. Thick shoulder-length auburn hair, amber eyes, high cheek bones with fine facial features and Angelina Jolie lips. He was getting excited just looking at her. He wondered what their children would look like.

"You keep staring at me. Is it because you think I'm beautiful?"

"You are beautiful. In fact, you're gorgeous."

Her bluntness surprised him, but didn't bother him. He liked her confidence and directness.

"Must be my Swedish heritage. By the way, my name is Beth Lundquist." She extended her hand and he shook it. He noticed the softness of her skin.

"Oh, I'm sorry. I'm Russell Parkhurst." She held a book in her left hand. "What's the book," he asked and pointed at it.

"Bible Quotations. I read it to relax before I dive." She opened it and started to read.

"'And the peace of God which passeth all understanding shall keep your hearts and minds through Jesus Christ.' Phillipians, Chapter - 4, Verse - 7.'"

"Wow, that's beautiful. I can see how that would relax you. I like to read the Bible, too. By the way, are you very religious?

"Not so much. I'm a Lutheran but I only go to church a couple of times a year."

"I'm Episcopal and I go to Bethesda-By-The-Sea every Christmas and Easter."

"Bethesda-By-The-Sea, what a pretty name for a church. Where is it?"

"In Palm Beach. That's where I live."

"Where's Palm Beach?"

"It's less than an hour from here - north on I-95," he said and pointed with his arm. This is good he thought. If she were a fortune hunter, she'd know Palm Beach.

"I notice you're carrying a notebook," she said looking at his hand. "Are you a reporter?"

"Sort of. I'm doing a story on this event for the Palm Beach Courant. Maybe we can make it a profile on you."

She moved closer to him - so close he could feel the heat from her body. She told him she grew up in Tallahassee where her father taught math at Florida State University. She had graduated from FSU with a Bachelor's degree in Education. She now worked part-time as a teacher and when her diving career was over she hoped to get her Master's Degree and teach high school math.

This was better than he anticipated. Not only was she beautiful, she was educated and intelligent.

Russell realized he was sweating and wiped his brow. She made him nervous.

"We seem to have a lot in common," he said.

"We do?"

"Well, we - we," he stammered, "both like to read the Bible but we only go to church twice a year and we're both athletes."

"Oh!" Beth seemed surprised. "What's your sport?"

"Well, tennis is my best sport. I've won some local championships and some sanctioned tournaments." An exaggeration, but he was trying to establish a commonality, though there really wasn't much of one and he knew it.

She stared at him with skepticism.

"Diving right now is my whole life. I'm working hard to make the U.S. National Team and go to the Rio Olympics."

"That's great," Russell replied with enthusiasm. "I've never been to Brazil. Maybe I'll go and cheer you on."

Beth seemed surprised. "You can take time off like that?"

"Sure. I'm a realtor and make my own hours and I just inherited three million dollars so I can easily afford it." He bit his lip. He wished he hadn't said that. A Palm Beach reflex, he thought, talking about money. He was trying too hard with her, but the whole experience excited him. This was his first time at bat and he thought he'd hit a home run."

"You'd better make your hotel reservations and buy your tickets to the games soon." She stared at him oddly.

"You know, there's no guarantee I'll make the team."

"Oh, you will. You will. I'm sure of it. I have great faith in you."

Beth now looked at him in disbelief. Russell knew he'd overdone it. She might wonder about him now, but that was okay. Yes, he thought, I guess I am a narcissist and always feel a sense of entitlement.

"I'm afraid we're going to have to cut this short," she said. "The bus is leaving for the motel."

"Oh, okay. Where are you staying?"

"At the La Quinta in Deerfield Beach."

"That's quite a hike, but it's on the way to Palm Beach. Maybe we could have dinner this evening and continue the conversation."

Beth hesitated. "I guess it's okay," she finally said.

"What's your room number?"

"I can't remember." She looked around. "What's our room number, Maizie," she shouted to another diver standing at the end of the bench. She was chatting with one of the male divers.

She gave Russell a nasty look before answering, "304."

"Seven o'clock sound good?"

Again Beth hesitated. "It's fine. I'll see you later."

That evening Russell dressed carefully. He chose a Lacoste blue polo shirt that matched his eyes and expensive Armani jeans.

After buying a dozen roses he got in his red Jaguar convertible and drove to the motel. On the way he thought where they might eat. Probably at the Town Center Mall after some window shopping. If Beth saw something she liked, he would offer to buy it. This would be an interesting test. Would she let him buy her an expensive gift? He was willing to buy anything, but if she chose something over $100 he would feel she was taking advantage. But she might refuse his offer to pay.

Russell entered the motel and strode to the elevator. Room 304 was at the end of the hall. He was about to knock when he noticed the door was slightly ajar. Why not surprise her, he thought. He pushed the door open and looked inside. Beth and Maizie were lying naked on one of the beds. Maizie was on top and her arms encircled Beth. They were French kissing.

Russell was stunned. He removed the paper from the roses and raised his arm as if to throw them. He wanted the thorns to scratch their naked bodies. Then he changed his mind and let the bouquet drop to the floor.

"'Who can find a virtuous woman? For her price is far above rubies. Proverbs Chapter - 31, Verse - 10.'" He spat out the words, turned and left. He heard the loud laughter from the girls as he slammed the door.

BEWARE THE COUGAR'S CLAWS

Jessica DiFranco sat at her dressing table and looked into her three-way mirror. She liked what she saw. Her skin was smooth, her brown hair lustrous, her blue eyes sparkled, but her mouth was turned down at the corners. She was a widow. Her husband Sam had died almost two years previously and now she was not only alone but lonely. She had to get over it, she told herself. Mourning two years was enough.

A small-town girl from Maumee, Ohio, Jessica had met Sam in New York when she was a gypsy - a dancer in Broadway musicals. Sam was an angel - a backer of Broadway plays and since she was dancing in *October Morn*, a play he was backing, he introduced himself. She liked him immediately and he liked her. Yes, he was much older and maybe, as some of her friends suggested, she was looking for a father figure. She could hardly remember her own father. He'd left home when she was four and she was raised by her mother who worked as a waitress at a local diner. Her mother was always involved with men she'd meet at work. They were usually crude and vulgar and often there were loud arguments and fights that sometimes became physical.

Jessica retreated from this turmoil into dance which she loved. Tap, jazz, modern, even ballet, she could do them all and she was good. Long-legged and extremely limber, when her teacher told her she could have a career in dance she worked even harder to master the steps. When she was eighteen she hopped a Greyhound bus to New York and found immediate employment as a Broadway dancer.

She loved dancing, but she was more interested in getting married and raising a family with Sam. When she was a child she remembered listening to Bobby Goldsboro on a local country radio station. The song was *Watching Scotty Grow* and the first time she heard it she cried. It told a story of a happy family watching their son grow up. That's what she wanted, a happy family atmosphere, and that's what Sam offered.

He pursued her avidly with flowers and expensive gifts, but friends warned her he was connected to the Mob. Jessica didn't care. He was always a gentleman around her, never cursing or acting crude, but early on she realized he didn't like questions about who he was or what he did. He was a businessman, he told her, and that was all she knew. He never discussed his work and when he said he was going on a business trip she didn't ask where or why.

Their daughter Donna was Jessica's main concern. She made sure she had everything she needed and was shielded from anything unpleasant. The one serious argument Jessica had with Sam was the time he invited some of his friends over for a poker night. They were loud, smoked smelly cigars and used vulgar language. Jessica asked Sam to take the game elsewhere and that was the last poker night in the DiFranco household.

When Sam developed cancer and was bedridden for two years, Jessica stayed by his side most of the day. She was heartbroken when he finally passed.

There was a large funeral at St. Edwards and a lot of the attendees Jessica had never seen before. Huge floral wreaths covered the altar and the pastor performed a Requiem High Mass.

There was a commotion outside the church when some of the men objected to the van parked across the street. A camera inside the van was aimed at the mourners as they left the church.

Jessica struggled with her life after Sam died. She played tennis and bridge twice a week. Occasionally she was asked to cocktail parties, but she felt alone and for the first time in her life she felt the need for male companionship. Just forty-two, sex for her had never been important. But now she began to fantasize about having sex with some of the men she met on a casual basis.

Her tennis partner Jill suggested she try the Island Grill. Jessica had never been interested in meeting men in bars. When she lived in New York there were always suitors hovering about: producers, directors, stage managers, choreographers, even stage-door johnnies, but she wasn't interested. She knew what she wanted and had found it with Sam.

She was skeptical about the Island Grill, but decided to try it. She thought about inviting her friend Jill, but decided against it. Going alone would give her a better chance to meet men. With a friend she would have to make conversation.

She arrived early at the Island Grill and found one of the last seats at the bar. Many men and women of all ages milled about. The noise and the crush was intense. Jessica ordered a dry martini and shrimp cocktail and looked in the mirror at the patrons behind her.

Suddenly a familiar face appeared next to her. "Where have you been all my life, gorgeous." It was Frank Keenan, a former New York City Police Department detective who had just divorced one of her tennis partners. "So you've stopped grieving and you're out on the hunt."

Thick-bodied and red-faced, he was full of mularkey. It occurred to her that if she got involved with Frank, he would grill her about Sam - who his friends were, what sort of business he was involved in. Not that she knew much, but she was sure he still had friends on the Force who would be curious about Sam.

"Just stopped in for a quick drink, Frank."

"You know I've always been madly in love with you." His blue eyes were bloodshot, his speech slurred, and angry-looking veins sprouted from his nose.

"Look, Frank, I'm just not interested." She turned away and sipped her martini. Suddenly she realized she had to break with her past. She could no longer be Mrs. Sam DiFranco. It would raise too many questions. She had to learn to be Jessica DiFranco.

She finished her shrimp cocktail, paid the bill, and got up to go.

"Leaving so soon? Have one on me." It was one of the bartenders. Tall and blond, he had a beautiful smile and his eyes crinkled at the corners. He looked like a California lifeguard. Jessica felt a stirring within and her heart beat faster.

"Can I take a rain check," she said as their eyes locked.

"I'm here every day but Monday," he replied still smiling. She quickly got up and pushed her way to the door. When she reached the exit she turned and looked back. He was still staring at her.

On the way home she tried to understand what had happened. The bartender was so young - he couldn't have been more than twenty-five. Why did she react to him in such an unusual way? He certainly was a break from her past. He didn't know who her husband had been. He wouldn't ask a lot of questions. It was clear to Jessica he was interested in her, but was she interested in him?

She was sure her friends would laugh at her, calling her a cougar and cradle robber, but she wouldn't care. Ever since she'd left Maumee, she'd been independent, not caring what anyone said.

She waited three days before returning to the Island Grill. As she sat down, the bartender appeared and placed a dry martini in front of her.

"I think this is your drink of choice," he said and smiled. "I'm Josh Fowler and I think I owe you one."

"I'm Jessica DiFranco. Nice to meet you."

"I hope you stay longer tonight. You left so quickly last time." He was charming and probably clever, Jessica thought. She wondered if he treated other customers in the same way.

The bar was crowded and the noise overpowering. Jessica left after one more martini. When she arrived home her phone was ringing.

"Hi. It's Josh. I hope you don't mind me calling you. You left without saying good-bye."

"It was too noisy for me. I don't know how you stand it."

"I agree. Conversation is difficult. Maybe we could meet someplace where it's quiet."

Here it comes, she thought. Not that she didn't expect him to ask her out. Now she was faced with a dilemma and she didn't know what to do.

"I don't know, Josh. I think I'm a little old for you."

"Age is just a number. I don't care how old you are. When I saw you, I was immediately attracted to you."

"I'm sorry, Josh. I want to think about it." She explained she was a widow and had not dated since her husband's death.

"Oh, okay. I understand. Well, I look forward to seeing you again at the Grill."

Jessica pondered her problem. Cougars were everywhere, but at age forty-two she didn't feel she was a cougar. If she was going to have an affair, now was a good time. Donna was away at boarding school. Palm Beach was crowded with tourists. So when they went out they wouldn't be so visible.

He was young and knew nothing about her or Sam. So he wouldn't ask questions about her past. This was probably the best reason to get involved with Josh.

The next time she saw Josh, she agreed to meet him for dinner at Tina's in City Place. Jessica wore a blue cocktail dress and emerald jewelry. Josh was waiting when she arrived. The maitre d' took them to a table in the front of the dining room. Jessica was amazed they weren't placed in the back of the room, but it occurred to her he probably thought they were mother and son. She looked carefully at Josh. She could be his mom, she thought.

"You look very beautiful tonight as always, Jessica," Josh said as he pulled her chair out.

"You know I'm old enough to be your mother," she said, curious to how he would react.

He broke into a loud laugh. "Well, you sure don't look like my mom. Oh, come on, let's forget this age stuff. I told you the minute I saw you I was attracted to you."

Jessica frowned. "This is the first date I've been on since my husband died two years ago. I just feel a little uneasy. I think you can understand that."

They ordered drinks and toasted. Josh explained he had recently returned from Afghanistan and he'd been working at the Grill for three months. He told Jessica he didn't have a girl friend and she was the first woman he'd gone out with from the Grill.

She had to accept his story. There was no point in ascribing ulterior motives to Josh. It was best to enjoy each other's company, stop doubting him and let things happen.

Dinner was fun. They ordered more drinks and a bottle of wine to complement their steaks. Jessica felt so comfortable that she invited Josh back to her house for a nightcap.

When the bill came she opened her purse and started rummaging around for her credit cards. "My treat," she said.

"Absolutely not." Josh stood up, removed a thick billfold from his pocket, and tossed a hundred-dollar bill on the table. Jessica's purse was still open and Josh looked inside. "Is that a gun?"

"Yes, it's a one-shot Derringer my husband gave me. He was away a lot and I was alone. I still carry it. I'm not sure why. Bet you saw a lot of guns in Afghanistan," she said somewhat defensively.

"I guess I did." He seemed upset.

When they walked into her home Josh seemed awed. It was a large Spanish-styled home in the estate section. It was set back from the street and had a swimming pool in the backyard.

It was warm for a February night and Jessica suggested a swim. "I don't have trunks," Josh said somewhat surprised.

"Well, wear your briefs. I'll be right down," she said as she climbed the stairs. She returned a few minutes later in a pink bikini and led him outside. She was impressed by his muscular physique.

The air was soft and slightly humid. The stars shone brightly. She felt like a teenager, full of high spirits. "Come on," she said and dove at the deep end.

He followed her in. She started to splash him in a playful manner. He splashed her back and then grabbed her hands so she'd stop. Jessica stared into his blue eyes. Suddenly he put his arms around her and kissed her passionately. It felt like a bolt of lightning passing through her body. As he pulled her close, she felt the hardness of his muscles and the softness of his skin. She found it hard to breathe and suggested they go inside.

"Come on upstairs and dry off," she said and laughed. They walked into the bedroom and she pulled Josh down on top of her. It was like sinking into a warm whirlpool. He kissed her face and then started kissing the rest of her body. She quivered and her heart seemed like it was going to burst through her chest. She had never felt such excitement before.

When it was over Jessica started to cry.

"What's the matter?"

"I don't know. It's just been such a long time. I think I've been dead emotionally until now." She reached over and kissed him gently.

Jessica was in love and had never felt so ecstatic. She and Josh became inseparable. They went on a binge of youthful activities. They danced, they sang, they picnicked, they frolicked on the beach, they went horseback riding. They even went to Disney World.

Jessica realized she was not reliving her childhood, but doing all the things she had never done as a child. Understanding the dynamics of the affair gave her power and insight. Instead of foolishly fantasizing, it would lead to marriage and another family. She accepted the fact it would end and only hoped they would remain friends.

But she wondered how she would tell her daughter Donna who was coming home from Choate for Spring Break. She would probably think her mother an old fool, but she didn't care. Donna would have to accept Josh. Just sixteen, Jessica thought she might be setting a bad example for Donna, but so what? The kids today were sexually aware and were always talking about hooking up. Donna favored Sam with olive skin, a prominent nose, and like Sam had a quiet manner. A good student, when all her friends from Palm Beach Day went off to boarding school Donna followed. Jessica would have preferred she stayed home and gone to Palm Beach High, but now with Josh always around she was glad Donna was away at school.

When she told Donna she was having an affair with a much younger man, Donna looked skeptical. "You know, mom, my best friend Cindy told me all the girls talk behind my back about dad. They say he was a big time mobster and at his funeral the Palm Beach Police wrote down the license plate numbers of those attending the funeral. Now, from what you tell me, everyone will be talking behind my back about you."

When Jessica explained why she was involved with Josh and how the relationship was under her control, Donna softened. "Wow, go for it mom, you deserve to have some fun."

They hugged each other and then went off to Worth Avenue to shop.

The next day Josh came by and met Donna. Jessica noticed her eyes widen. She later commented, "He seems nice."

Even though Donna was home, Jessica kept to the same routine. On Monday and Thursday afternoons she played doubles at Seaview and on Tuesdays and Fridays she played bridge with her tennis partners.

She went to the courts the following Monday and they began to play, but as often happens in South Florida a sudden shower interrupted them and play ended.

Jessica drove home and was surprised to see Josh's car parked in the driveway. They hadn't planned to meet but sometimes he came by unexpectedly.

When she walked in the front door she heard laughter from upstairs. She assumed it was Donna entertaining school friends. She put her keys on the hall table and glanced at the mail. The noises upstairs suddenly changed to sounds of joy. Jessica tiptoed up the stairs quickly and eased open the door to Donna's bedroom. The scene stunned her. Josh and Donna were naked in bed. Furious and blind with rage, Jessica removed her Derringer from her handbag and aimed the pistol at Josh's leg. The shot went off and Josh grabbed his leg and started writhing. Donna became hysterical and screamed.

Jessica went ice cold. "Let's everybody calm down," she said in a quiet tone. "You've just committed statutory rape, Josh, which should land you in prison for a long term. Donna probably lied to you, but she's only seventeen. And as for you, young lady, I'm going to lie about your age and you're going in the Army. Maybe then you'll learn a little respect."

She turned to Josh who was examining his wound. "Josh, I never want to see you again. As for pressing charges against me, forget it. I don't think you want to be accused of statutory rape. However, luckily for you, my husband knew a doctor who can treat your wound and not report it to the police."

Donna and Josh stared at Jessica as she casually put the Derringer back in her purse.

TWO-UPMANSHIP

Curtis Fager wanted to sell his Palm Beach condo because he was tired of Palm Beach life. Just fifty years old, he missed New York where he was born and had lived forty years. He missed the energy and excitement of the Big Apple. He missed his friends, the cultural opportunities, the buzz of the Big City.

He still owned his 15th row, forty-yard line season tickets to the Giants football games - he would never give them up - and he still had lady friends who he felt would welcome his return.

Palm Beach was for retirees who liked to sit in the sun and play golf. He was too young, too energetic. A money manager, he had clients in New York and Palm Beach and now with Skype he could service them without travel, but he couldn't service his girlfriend Darla with Skype.

She was a problem. When he announced his move to New York, Darla was upset. He tried to pacify her by telling her he would fly to Palm Beach on weekends.

"A lot of people do that," he assured her.

"Then why sell your condo," she parried.

"So I can stay with you," he countered.

She gave him a nasty look. The relationship had become strained. Another reason to move back to New York, he thought. They had dated for five years, as long as he had lived in Palm Beach. Now she was pressing him to marry her - something he did not want to do since he had already been unhappily married and divorced.

Curtis' unit was in the Blenheim, a highrise condo on the Intracoastal with a view of the ocean from the upper floors, but he lived on the fifth floor in a small two-bedroom, two-bath. He thought he could list it for $850,000, but the realtor convinced him that $650,000 was more realistic.

He didn't like the realtor, Olivia Tattersall, though she came with high recommendations. Extremely well turned out in a Chanel suit and bag, Ferragamo pumps, and Hermes scarf, she had long blond hair and a recent facelift. Almost a cliche, she spoke with an affected accent and used the word elegant in every other sentence.

"We'll have to stage this place," she told him as if his apartment was a theater set and not up to her high standards, "which means you'll have to move out."

"Well, I'm going away this summer, but I don't know exactly when. Why don't we wait until fall."

She gave him a thoughtful look. "Why don't we make it a pocket listing for the summer?"

"What's a pocket listing?"

"It means I can show the unit, but only to friends and clients who may want to buy it or look for comparables, but it won't be in the MLS and, of course, I'll call you first to make sure you're not at home."

Curtis was confused. "So when does the listing start?"

"Now, as I explained." She acted like she was talking to a school boy. "It won't be in the MLS until September."

He raised his eyebrows and stared at her. "So this is a nine-month listing?"

"Not really. Look, I'm here now. My time is valuable, as is yours I'm sure. Why don't we get this out of the way today. I've brought the paperwork with me."

She was so insufferable. Oh, well, why not, he thought. Let's get this thing moving before I change my mind.

As soon as she left he thought he'd made a mistake. His condo was at the low end by Palm Beach standards and he was sure she specialized in high-end properties.

At first he didn't want to move out, but then he thought about it. It was late June - he always went north in the summer to cool off, usually to Newport or East Hampton. Darla had already taken her vacation, so he would have time away from her, time to look up old girlfriends and find a place to live in New York.

But where to go? He had seen an ad in Southern Living magazine for a cruise to Newfoundland. His grandfather had a fishing camp in Newfoundland which he was always talking about. He even invited Curtis one summer, but his mother convinced him he wouldn't like it. Lots of flies and nothing to do but fish during the day and watch his grandfather's buddies get drunk at night. Still, Newfoundland sounded interesting, as did the rest of the cruise: Montreal, Quebec City, Sept Isles, St. Pierre, and Miquelon. Why not? He'd never heard of the ship *SS QUEBEC*, or the cruiseline Canadian National, but it didn't matter. He was going for the ports, not the cruise experience. Newport and East Hampton were okay, but it was time to do something different.

He planned his itinerary with care. He would take the AutoTrain from Sanford to Lorton, then spend a few days in New York and look up former girlfriends, then drive to Lake Placid, a place he'd never seen, but his parents always talked about the Lake Placid Club long since closed. From there it was an easy drive to Montreal.

Curtis was shocked when he saw the ship docked at its pier in Montreal. The other cruise ships dwarfed the SS QUEBEC. Only 300 feet long, it was really no more than a large glorified yacht. When he opened the door to his cabin he was even more surprised - a small single bed placed against the wall in a tiny room. His balcony, if you could call it that, was so small there was barely room to sit. On his bed was a pamphlet welcoming him aboard and a passenger list. Curtis thought passenger lists were from the past. Didn't everybody want to remain anonymous?

When he scanned the list he noticed there was a large Florida contingent: Orlando, Miami, Fort Lauderdale and Tallahassee were represented. There was even a couple from Palm Beach - Toni and Wilson Peete. He didn't recognize the name, but felt sure they knew many of the same Palm Beachers.

He laid down on the bed, stared at the ceiling and wondered what he was doing on this cruise. This ship was not for him - no swimming pool, no spa, no casino, no orchestra, no dance floor, no entertainment. They did have port lecturers who would undoubtedly give talks, but at $750 per diem the price seemed outrageous. He was used to Crystal Cruises which had a similar price point.

Lunch was announced on the PA system and he walked down the narrow stairs into the dining room. It was open seating and he sat at a table for eight. All of his tablemates were older, some of them in their seventies or eighties he guessed. He looked at the table setting - red paper placemats, white china without a logo that looked like it came from the Automat, and a centerpiece of plastic flowers.

People at the table introduced themselves and engaged in animated conversation. They talked about small ship cruising, which this certainly was, and how much they liked it.

Curtis quickly realized that aside from the itinerary, this cruise was about getting to know your fellow passengers. He had thought he might be lonely on this cruise. Now he wondered if there was going to be too much interaction.

He looked around the dining room. To his amazement everyone was old, white, and probably rich. New money, he thought; not flashy, vulgar Palm Beach new money, but new money from the hinterlands.

At the table next to him he noticed two women who looked like identical twins; long brown hair, broad faces, brown eyes, capped teeth. He couldn't stop staring. They'd both had a lot of work done on their faces. At the very least, they had cheek bone and chin implants and their lips were collagened or somehow had been sculpted. Their appearance was striking, but what did they look like before surgery?

One of the women noticed his stare and smiled at him. He smiled back and vowed to meet them after lunch. He wondered how old they were, but it was impossible to tell because their skin had been pulled so tight at the neck and collagen inserted around the eyes.

That evening they served cocktails and hors d'oeuvres in the St. Lawrence room, the main passenger lounge. Drinks were free and all top-shelf.

Curtis ordered a glass of Cabernet and found the identical twins who were both talking on their iPhones. He sat down beside them and waited until they put their phones down.

"I noticed you're always talking on your cellphones."

"We're realtors," one of them said.

"And we're always doing business," the other finished the sentence.

"I'm Debbie," one said.

"And I'm Sally Frank," the other girl continued.

Curtis introduced himself and asked where they lived.

"West Palm Beach," Debbie replied.

Curtis explained that he lived in Palm Beach and how he had just listed his condo and was unhappy with the realtor.

"Well, you can always cancel the listing, you know," Debbie said.

"I didn't know that," Curtis interjected.

"But the realtor has to agree to it and a lot of times they won't."

"Do you know Olivia Tattersall," Curtis asked.

They both chuckled. "Everyone knows Olivia. She's legendary."

"Legendary for what?"

"Well, she's very Palm Beach, very elegant, very snobbish."

"Well, I don't like her and now you tell me I can get rid of her if I want."

"Well, you can," Debbie said, "but she has to agree and I don't think she will."

"Well, I think she will," Curtis thrust his jaw out and answered with force.

After cocktails they sat down to dinner at a table for ten. Curtis was impressed with the twins. They had excellent people skills and were consistently upbeat. They agreed to take his listing if he could get Olivia to cancel.

That evening's entertainment was a lecture on Quebec City, the port they would visit the next day. Curtis felt better about the cruise, the ship, and his shipmates. It was just a different experience and he had to get used to it.

By the time the ship returned to Montreal, Curtis and the twins had become friends. He told them he would contact them as soon as he returned to Palm Beach. They were flying back, but he didn't expect to return until the end of August. Instead he rescheduled his AutoTrain reservation, drove to New York City to meet with a client, and got on the AutoTrain the next day.

When he returned to the Blenheim he asked the doorman if the realtor had shown the apartment in his absence. The man looked at the log and told him no. Curtis started to seethe. He was going to make this so unpleasant for Olivia that she would beg him to cancel the listing.

He entered his apartment and looked around. Olivia had rearranged the furniture and put bowls of faux fruit on some of the tables. She had even added some scent that made the place smell like a woman's boudoir.

Curtis was furious. He threw the fruit out, put the furniture back the way it had been, and flushed the sachets down the toilet.

He checked his telephone messages and found that Olivia had called him the day before. Could she have a buyer, he wondered. He called her.

"Great news," she gushed. "I have a buyer and he wants to close in three weeks. Can I fax you the contract?"

"What's the asking price?"

"$600,000."

"But it's listed for $650,000."

"You want to sell it, don't you?" She sounded almost seductive.

Why not, Curtis thought. It's time to get out of here. "Okay. Send it over and I'll look at it." He gave Olivia his fax number and hung up.

Nobody uses faxes anymore, he thought. He couldn't remember the last time he'd used his machine. He turned it on and searched for paper. He found a small bundle in the bottom drawer of his desk, but he couldn't remember whether to put it on top or on the bottom of the machine. He heard the phone ring and hurriedly shoved the paper on top. His fax beeped, but nothing happened. He changed the paper to the bottom. The phone rang again, the machine beeped, but again nothing happened. The next time he picked up the phone.

"Look, I can't get this thing to work. Can't you email me?"

"I can," she sounded irritated, "but you'll have to sign it and bring it to my office. I'm terribly busy so you'll have to bring it right away; and if I'm not in, leave it with my secretary."

She was annoying, he thought. He turned his laptop on and waited for the contract for sale and purchase agreement to appear. It was twelve pages long.

On the first page Curtis noticed on the deposit line there was $6,000 written in. That's one percent, he thought. That's ridiculous. That's hardly earnest money. He closed his computer and called the Franks.

Debbie answered and he told her about the offer.

"Don't accept it," she practically shouted. "One percent is ridiculous. Ten percent is the minimum. If it's only one percent, they can walk. Then you split the deposit with the realtor. Sounds as if she's playing games. Are all of your appliances in working order?"

"Well, sort of. The AC is awfully loud. There's something loose inside. Some of the neighbors have complained."

"Then you'll have to replace it. That's $5,000. I suggest you stall. Tell Olivia you want twenty percent down. Have them do the inspections now and then sell the unit as-is."

"I'll do better than that. I'll get her to cancel the listing. I'll call you back in a few minutes."

This was going to be easy he thought. He dialed Olivia's number.

"This contract is unacceptable," Curtis said in a strong voice.

"What's wrong with it?"

"This one percent deposit is an insult."

"Well, it was my idea."

"It's a bad idea."

There was a pause. "According to the State of Florida ..."

"I don't give a fuck what the State of Florida says. One percent is an insult and this is not a legitimate offer."

He heard a sigh. "Mr. Fager, I have been buying and selling real estate in Florida for the last twenty-five years."

"So have I," he shouted, "and I'm afraid you've misled your fucking client."

"I really don't like your language, Mr. Fager."

"And I don't like your language or you, for that matter. You're a lousy realtor. Why don't we just cancel this listing?" There was a pause.

"I'll email you a cancellation form and you can sign it and drop it off at my office."

He hung up and called the Franks. "It's a done deal. I got Olivia to cancel. Come on over with a contract and I'll sign it."

In a short while both Franks came over. "How did you do it," Debbie asked.

"It was easy," he said with a smile. "Care for a glass of champagne?"

He poured three glasses and they toasted. "What's life without a little strife," Curtis said and laughed.

ROMAN FEVER

A Play in 3 Acts

THE PLAYERS

PAM FOLEY - Winifred's daughter

WINIFRED FOLEY - Pam's mother

LAWRENCE FOLEY - Pam's uncle

JACK FOLEY - Pam's brother

DAVID HENRIQUES - Pam's Italian lover

TAYLOR CARROLL - Pam's Palm Beach suitor

ACT I Scene 1

(Living room of a Spanish style home in Palm Beach. It is a large room with bright chintz covered furniture and a sandstone fireplace. Winifred and Pam are talking. Winifred is petite, slender with brown hair, blue eyes, and high cheekbones. She is almost beautiful but a bit too stern. She is embroidering a sampler. Pam is overweight with a blocky body and dyed blond curly hair; big boned, broad shouldered. She does not resemble her mother.)

(The time is June 1962.)

PAM

(Enters) Oh, Mom, Mom, Kenny just dumped me. (She goes to mother and they hug.) He said he never wants to see me again - We're finished.

WINIFRED

Oh, darling. I'm so sorry, but maybe you're better off without him.

PAM

Oh, Mom, I love him so much. He was so kind and caring. Then all of a sudden he changed and said the most terrible things to me; that I was fat and lazy and clinging, that he was embarrassed to be seen with me. Then I tried to get back the $1,000 I'd loaned him and he just laughed at me. Just try to get it back, he said.

WINIFRED

What do you expect from a used car salesman, and not a very good one! I think you can do better than that. I'd never told you this before but your uncle had him investigated and it seems he fathered a child out of wedlock and his wages were being garnished for nonpayment of child support.

Pam

That doesn't surprise me. But, Mom, you don't love a man because he's perfect. Kenny has many good qualities. He's handsome with a great sense of humor.

Winifred

But I don't think he's appropriate for you. You always seem to pick these guys who are no-gooders. Remember that business with the lifeguard at the Bougainvillea Club? Your father got him fired, but the damage was already done. Everybody at the club knew about it and for a couple of weeks that's all anybody talked about. I felt the stares whenever I went there.

And then there was that dance instructor character. He was slightly more presentable, but his reputation for sleeping with his students was well known.

I wish you'd find a nice boy at the club, or maybe one of your ex-school mates. Someone who fits in more.

Pam

(Flops on couch.) I've told you, Mom. All the so-called nice boys, boys at the club - former schoolmates - they don't want anything to do with me. Let's face it. I'm a large lady and most of the girls at the club are practically anorexic.

Some actually are anorexic. Remember Patty Barnes? She must weigh 90 pounds and she runs in these marathons. Can you believe it?

Winifred

You could lose a few pounds, but you're still attractive enough. Maybe we should give a little cocktail party and dinner at the club, let everyone know you're back in circulation.

Pam

I don't feel up to it, Mom. I know I'm going to miss Kenny. He was a large part of my life. (Starts weeping again.) We discussed getting married. If he'd asked me, I would have married him.

Winifred

(Aghast) You would have! (Starts pacing, looking concerned) Well, you should go down to the club this weekend before it closes for the season and tell everyone you know you're back in circulation.

Pam

They're having some sort of children's swimming meet. All the young parents will be there.

Winifred

Well, they have brothers and sisters, don't they? Maybe you could help out, do some officiating, help with the timers. I don't know. Just so everyone knows you're rid of Kenny and you're looking.

Pam

But I'm not looking, Mom. I can't just forget Kenny like that (snaps fingers). It's going to take time, lots of time.

Winifred

Well, you can concentrate on your job at Neiman Marcus.

Pam

You know I hate it there. All those la-di-da bitchy women who shop there and the women who work there aren't much better. I prefer the company of men and always have.

Winifred

(Rolls eyes) I'm aware of that. I remember when you tried being a Sterling representative and you did those in-home jewelry parties. I thought you'd be good at that with your outgoing personality. You gave one party and you told me you would never give another because you couldn't stand women in groups.

Women in groups is what Palm Beach is all about. All the cultural events, all the charity balls, all the art openings are run by women in groups. Let's face it. Women in groups run Palm Beach. (Stops pacing and turns to Pam) Well, you can always take the real estate license test again. That should take your mind off Kenny.

Pam

I got so nervous before I took the test the last time. That's why I failed. Now I'll have to take one of those cram courses to prepare for the next test.

Winifred

(Sits beside Pam and clasps her hands) When you get your real estate license, you'll meet a lot of men, nice men, substantial men, men with money and class. That's the kind of person who lives in Palm Beach and that's the kind of man you should be looking for. Not these lifeguards and used car salesmen. There's no future with them. They may have been attentive and loving, but you've got to think of the future. You're 23 now, still young, but I think you'd be better off married. Then you can feel more confident, more secure.

(Looks at her wristwatch) Speaking of women in groups, I've got to go to a meeting of the Four Arts.

(Offstage door opens and closes and Uncle Lawrence Foley walks in. He is in his fifties, red-faced and nattily attired in blue blazer, pink polo shirt, and lime green ascot.

LAWRENCE

Well, what have we here? It looks like a real mother-daughter to me. I stopped by to return this book about Palm Beach. It was okay, but he name dropped all over the place and I was disappointed he didn't mention me.

WINIFRED

(Taking the book from Lawrence) You could have at least knocked. We're having a serious conversation.

PAM

Here he is, Mr. Palm Beach - the answer to every maiden's prayer.

LAWRENCE

I don't know any maidens. Are there any maidens in Palm Beach? If there are, I haven't met them.

WINIFRED

Why would you? You only prey on widows and divorcees.

LAWRENCE

You forget, I perform a service. These widows and divorcees are lonely and they need escorts for cocktail parties, art openings, charity balls. I provide the service. I don't prey on them. You've seen the Foley coat of arms in my home. You remember the motto below the knight's shield - "Ut Prosim," that "I may serve."

WINIFRED

Sometimes I wonder what kind of service you perform and if you're being paid.

LAWRENCE

Enough about me! What is this serious conversation about? Not about your job, I hope.

PAM

No. I'm resigning from Neiman Marcus. I have a new career. I'm getting my real estate license.

LAWRENCE

(Laughs) Everybody in Palm Beach has a real estate license. Even I have mine. Pretty soon there will be so many realtors we'll all be selling to each other.

WINIFRED

Look, Lawrence. We're having a serious conversation about marriage. Pam wants to get married, but her boyfriend just walked away.

LAWRENCE

Are you sure you want to get married, Pam?

PAM

Of course I'm sure. Why wouldn't I want to get married?

LAWRENCE

Oh, I don't know. For starters, forty percent of today's marriages end in divorce. Do you want to be a statistic? The whole idea of marriage seems dated to me. Think about it. My mother used to cook from scratch, clean the house, wash and iron the family's clothes, mother the children, be a helpmate to my dad. She was functional. She served many purposes.

Today women have careers. Labor saving devices have made all the household chores easier and now nannies have taken over child rearing. What's the point of marriage and why are you so eager to get married?

PAM

That's what we were talking about. I like men and I'd feel more comfortable if I was married.

LAWRENCE

Marriage is a contract, isn't it? If it is, why not make it a renewable contract? Every five years or so each party could have the option to renew it. If they choose not to, there should be no penalty and they can just say good-bye.

Of course it would put a lot of attorneys out of work, but so what?

WINIFRED

(Angrily) You're talking this way because you were never married.

LAWRENCE

Well, I never married because I never found the woman of my dreams.

But I'll tell you something else. When I joined the trust department of JP Morgan in New York, I met a lot of men and women who were always talking about Palm Beach. They all liked me because I only put them in conservative money-making investments. Then a lot of these trust-fund babies moved to Palm Beach. So when I retired from Morgan, I moved here. I found out that by then a lot of them were widowed or divorced and they welcomed me, literally with open arms. Since I had never been married, a lot of them thought I might be queer. But I showed them I wasn't.

WINIFRED

Oh, please. I'm tired of hearing about your conquests. Pam just got hurt by this no-good used car salesman. We're trying to find a more suitable guy for her. In your travels have you met anybody who would be right for Pam?

LAWRENCE

(Pauses) No one comes to mind, but I'll think about it.

WINIFRED

(Looks at her watch) Your brother Jack is coming home from Dartmouth tomorrow. Maybe he'll have some ideas. Please excuse me. I've got to get to that Four Arts meeting.

LAWRENCE

I'd like a word with you, Winifred. Let's go out in the garden. (They walk down stage and then a scrim of a garden drops behind them.)

WINIFRED

Haven't you said enough already? Sometimes I just don't understand you, Lawrence. Pam wants to get married. We're trying to get her married off and you make these ridiculous anti-marriage comments.

LAWRENCE

You know I was only kidding. Just having a little fun.

WINIFRED

Well, you sure fooled me and Pam thought you were being serious.

LAWRENCE

I know I've never been married and I make fun of the institution, but it's only because, as I said, I've never found the right woman. If I'd found her, I would have married her in a heart beat. I remember when James was courting you and I thought he was a very lucky man. I really envied him. You seemed to have everything - beauty, intelligence, class, especially class. Let's face it. The Foleys were a pretty rough bunch - drinkers, brawlers, gamblers. Not my brother James, though. He was quite a guy - big, strong, handsome with a winning smile. I was always weak and sickly, kind of like the Kennedy brothers. Jack's brother Joe was the shining light of the family until he got killed in World

War II. Then the mantel was passed to Jack. Now look, he's in the White House. I'm not comparing the Foleys to the Kennedys but we were just as much a political family as they are. My father and his father were Tammany Hall regulars and my dad was one of the so-called sachems, but we didn't stick with politics like the Kennedys, but your family, the Van Ingens, seemed to have all the qualities the Foleys lacked.

WINIFRED

I'm very surprised to hear you say all this. You were always making fun of me and my family.

LAWRENCE

You all seemed so high and mighty as if you were royalty and you always seemed to be looking down your nose at the Foleys.

WINIFRED

The Van Ingens have been around a lot longer than the Foleys, but we've had our share of black sheep.

LAWRENCE

Every family has black sheep, but let's face it, your family has more class than the Foleys.

WINIFRED

Is that so important?

LAWRENCE

Yes, I think so. When you have money, you want respect and class gives you respect.

WINIFRED

I'm not so sure. In our society, money counts more than class.

LAWRENCE

Yes, if you don't have money, then class doesn't matter. But in Palm Beach class is very important.

You think we could be members of the Bougainvillea and the Everglades Club if we didn't have class?

WINIFRED

I wish you'd remind Pam about this. She prefers boyfriends without class - life guards, masseurs, dance instructors, and now a used car salesman.

LAWRENCE

Don't worry. She'll see the light.

WINIFRED

I certainly hope so. I'm planning a surprise for her so she'll forget this no good used car salesman.

You know, I'm so sick of the Kennedys. That's all anyone talks about these days. It's usually some indiscretion of Jack's. Apparently he's like a dog in heat.

LAWRENCE

I wonder how Jackie feels about all this.

WINIFRED

She's apparently long-suffering. Her father was a notorious womanizer. So she's used to it. The public can't seem to get enough of her with her wispy little voice and retiring manner. She appears very petite and sensitive, but she's really a tough cookie. I remember when I saw her walking down Worth Avenue I was very surprised. She's much taller than people realize, about five feet ten inches with thick long legs and large feet. I think she's spent too much time horseback riding. She has a very clumpy walk.

LAWRENCE

She's been a big help to Jack. The public adores her. Every secretary and housewife copies her fashions - the Jackie look. Pillbox hats, Chanel suits, sheath dresses - you see them everywhere.

WINIFRED

Well, I don't copy her fashions.

LAWRENCE

Look at the dress you're wearing! It's a Lilly Pulitzer, isn't it?

WINIFRED

(Angrily) I was wearing these long before Jackie started wearing them. They say the Kennedys are going to be like the Bonapartes - it's going to be a dynasty. Have you heard the latest joke? Jack will have four more years, then Bobby will have eight, and Teddy will have eight, and by then it will be 1984.

LAWRENCE

Very amusing, but I'm very proud of our president and I think he's done a great job. He messed up the Bay of Pigs, but the American public forgave him because he took responsibility and admitted it was his fault.

WINIFRED

I'm still worried about Cuba. That tiny little pimple of a country thumbing its nose at us and now Castro is going to Russia. I think we'll have more trouble ahead. As Kennedy keeps saying, it's only ninety miles away.

LAWRENCE

Don't worry, the CIA will probably assassinate Castro and we'll invade the country correctly next time.

WINIFRED

I hope you're right, but I doubt it. Castro is a very slippery character. You know, he never sleeps in the same place for more than one night at a time. I hope the CIA can find him. (She looks at her wristwatch.) Look, I've got to get to that Four Arts meeting. Please be more supportive of Pam and her wish to be married. Oh, by the way, I have a surprise for you.

LAWRENCE

Of course I will be more supportive, but first tell me about this surprise you're planning.

WINIFRED

(Hesitates) I don't want to discuss it now.

LAWRENCE

Why not? Is it a state secret?

WINIFRED

Not exactly.

LAWRENCE

Then tell me.

WINIFRED

I'd rather not. You'll know about it when it happens.

Act I Scene 2

(The next day. The scene is the same and it is the cocktail hour. Winifred's son Jack sits on the sofa reading the Palm Beach Daily News. He is tall and thin, a slightly nerdish Ivy Leaguer with thick horn-rimmed glasses and short hair. Winifred walks in wearing a Lilly Pulitzer shift and Jack Rogers sandals. She goes to the bar and starts to mix a martini.)

WINIFRED

I've got a surprise for you Jack. v You're going to Rome.

JACK

I don't understand. What's the occasion.

WINIFRED

I don't know. I just thought it might be a nice interlude for you and your sister.

JACK

Do I have any say in this matter?

WINIFRED

(Testily) Well, if you don't want to go, I'll cancel the trip. I thought this would be a great opportunity for you. You've never been to Europe.

JACK

I assume you want me to chaperone Pam.

WINIFRED

Well, she's your sister. I thought you would want to escort her around.

JACK

(After a pause) Who is it this time?

WINIFRED

(Turns and glares at Jack) He's a used car salesman and, can you believe it, Pam wanted to marry him. Your uncle had him investigated and found out he had a child out of wedlock and is behind in his support payments. And Pam actually wanted to marry this guy.

JACK

(Smiling) Well, why not? At least he's doing something with his life. Would you rather she went out with layabouts and remittance men?

WINIFRED

Frankly, yes if they have breeding, good manners, and some semblance of backbone. (Looks plaintively at Jack)

JACK

You and Pam have always talked about marriage as if it were the Holy Grail. You have always been obsessed with marriage and you've always said it was the natural lifestyle. No wonder Pam wants to get married to anybody, no matter how inappropriate.

WINIFRED

Yes, I believe that marriage is the only natural state. Look at your Uncle Lawrence. Fifty-five years old, never married, and he carries on like he was cock of the walk. What a buffoon.

JACK

(Laughs) I think he's great. You don't seem to have much of a sense of humor about all this.

WINIFRED

I don't care what your uncle does, but I am concerned about Pam. Look, let's face it. She is rather large and ungainly in a society that values slimness. You know what they say - you can't be too rich or too thin.

JACK

I wish whoever coined that phrase - Elizabeth Arden or the Duchess of Windsor - had never said it. Most of the girls and women in Palm Beach firmly believe it to be true and now you have a lot of scarecrows wandering around Palm Beach.

And at the Bougainvillea Club, at least four, maybe five of the women there are anorexic. The irony is the rest of the country is fighting obesity, but in our little island paradise we have the opposite problem. (Gets up and pours himself a martini.)

WINIFRED

(Sighing) I wish Pam would marry someone who fits in and would settle down. All this catting around has to stop. If it continues, she'll ruin her reputation and then no one will want her. I worry about her a lot. She's not as strong as she used to be. You remember what happened when she was eighteen.

JACK

(Rolling eyes) How can I forget? She was as usual struggling with her weight and she went to that quack diet doctor who prescribed amphetamines - pep pills.
Pam overdosed and the pills caused a nervous breakdown.
Okay. So she recovered, but I think your relationship with her has been strained ever since.

WINIFRED

Your sister has always needed my help.

JACK

Mom, I've got to be honest with you. You always worry about Pam, but you never seem concerned about how I'm doing and you expect so much of me. I'm studying at Dartmouth for a Bachelor's degree in History and Pam is studying at Palm Beach Community College for an Associate's degree in Marketing. So expectations are lower for her. Yet you seem to coddle her.

WINIFRED

Oh, please. You're a man. You're supposed to be able to take care of yourself.

JACK

But you never even ask how I feel or if anything is bothering me.

WINIFRED

I'm not worried about you. You're smart. You should be able to handle every situation.

JACK

(Pauses) That's the kind of thing Dad used to say.

WINIFRED

Look, we all miss your father. I probably miss him more than you do, but we have to get on with our lives. Driving around here can be very dangerous, as he found out. I hope you're very careful.

JACK

I am.

WINIFRED

Now Pam has substituted Uncle Lawrence as a father figure. I'm not sure I approve. Your father was much more serious and dignified.

JACK

I think Uncle Lawrence is great. He has a sense of humor. Something we could use more of around here. You and Pam are much too serious. You both should lighten up. Getting married isn't the be all and end all that it used to be (pause).

WINIFRED

Do you ever think of getting married?

JACK

I'm not ready and there's always military service.

WINIFRED

Do you think you'll be drafted?

JACK

(Surprised) No, I'll probably get a student deferment. I may never serve. Besides, they're not drafting anyone now.

WINIFRED

Both your father and Uncle Lawrence served in World War II with distinction.

JACK

That was a different time and a different war. A just war and we were the good guys.

WINIFRED

And we're not the good guys now?

JACK

(Heatedly) No! We shouldn't even be there. They were supposedly to hold free elections when the French left, but they never held them. Anyhow, we have 12,000 so-called observers there now and Kennedy is no fool. He knows it's not our war and he's going to try to end it soon. De Gaulle warned him Viet Nam is a bottomless pit that will soak up men and materials.

WINIFRED

You really think we're going to leave? What about Diem and Madame Nhu and her husband?

JACK

(Heatedly) A bunch of corrupt fools and another reason to leave.

WINIFRED

I don't know where you get all of this information.

JACK

I'm a history major, remember! And a lot of the history professors at Dartmouth have friends in high places in Washington. So we get the inside scoop.

WINIFRED

Well, you're majoring in American history. Have you thought about your thesis yet?

JACK

Yes. And I'm going to concentrate on 19th Century politics in urban America.

WINIFRED

You're not going to write about Tammany Hall, I hope.

JACK

That's what I'm doing my thesis on.

WINIFRED

(Shocked) Your father is going to roll over in his grave. Why do you have to dig up all that dirt?

JACK

Are you kidding? Those guys were geniuses and no worse than the politicians today. They were opportunists who knew how to manipulate the system and they did it. I wish Dad had talked more about Tammany Hall. Maybe we would have kept the Foley name alive in politics instead of going into investment banking, trying to preserve and increase the family fortune. In my research I found out that Tammany Hall was no worse than the machine politics of other northeastern cities like Philadelphia or Boston, but Tammany got more publicity and the heirs of the Tammany politicos all felt politics was dirty and tainted.

But look at Boston and the Kennedys. They had some questionable dealings, but they stuck with politics and now John Kennedy is President. The Foleys could have done the same thing. I'm not saying we could have produced a president, but we had to be respectable and leave New York and move to Palm Beach. That's the trouble with the Irish - because of their rough backgrounds, they always want to be respectable. But now with Kennedy in the White House we've achieved respectability and acceptance. It's really a great achievement.

WINIFRED

Don't forget, my family was completely different from your father's. The Van Ingens settled in Manhattan in 1651 and we've had money for five generations. Respectability has never been an issue with us.

JACK

That's better than most of the old families we know. You've heard the expression: "Shirt sleeves to shirt sleeves in three generations."

WINIFRED

Well, you're the third generation on your father's side with money. I hope you don't end up in shirt sleeves.
But you'll probably teach at an Ivy League college and live somewhere in the Northeast.

Pam wants to stay here in Palm Beach; and if you're going to live in Palm Beach, you have to understand the rules and the values.

JACK

Our Palm Beach. The WASP Palm Beach. Have you noticed that our little group seems to be getting smaller and smaller, but the Palm Beach Jews seem to be more numerous.

WINIFRED

All the more reason we have to stick together.

JACK

I'm not so sure. We're already too inbred. Look at the faces of some of my friends - receding chins, button noses, dull eyes, pasty skin. I think an injection of new blood might be healthy.

WINIFRED

That's the trouble with these Ivy League schools and their liberal professors. They fill your head with a lot of claptrap. We are the true aristocrats of this country and have to set the standards for everyone else. These parvenus are all rude, pushy, ill bred, and ill mannered.

JACK

(Laughs) Don't you think people said the same thing about our ancestors? All the Palm Beachers we know have had money for at least three generations, but the nouveaux have energy and ideas. They don't just sit around their clubs and discuss social nuances. The whole thing is way too self-conscious.

WINIFRED

Are you quite finished? Look, I want you to chaperone Pam on this trip to Italy. I want her to enjoy herself and forget about this no-gooder.

JACK

How 19th Century! Send your daughter to Europe to forget an unhappy love affair. Sounds like something out of Edith Wharton or Henry James.

WINIFRED

I wish you'd be serious for a change.

JACK

I am being serious. When do we leave?

WINIFRED

In two weeks. I've made reservations at the Rome Excelsior for the first two nights and the last two nights of your stay. I thought you might want to tour in between. American Express in Rome can make reservations for you. Oh, and be sure to write me from time to time. If it's important, telephone me. I'm going to be in East Hampton, trying to forget about your sister.

(The front door opens and Pam enters. She has obviously been drinking.)

PAM

Talking about me, huh? Don't deny it. I can tell.
    (She flops on the sofa.) Yes, I've been drinking. Can you blame me? I'm trying to forget that shit who dumped me.

WINIFRED

Dear, we're talking about your trip to Italy. I have tickets for you and Jack. You're leaving for Rome next week. It's a great opportunity to forget him, have some fun, and soak up some culture.

PAM

Why would I want to go to Rome? No, I'm not going.

JACK

Oh, come on, Pam. A lot of Americans will be in Rome this summer and we'll have a lot of fun.

PAM

No, thanks. I'm staying here.

WINIFRED

This will give you a chance to forget Kenny and possibly meet a new man. Remember that movie we saw together - *Rome Adventure* with Suzanne Pleshette and Troy Donahue? Maybe you'll meet someone like Troy.

PAM

I doubt it, but I did like that movie. Rome seemed so beautiful and I guess there will be a lot of Americans there this summer.

WINIFRED

I know you're going to enjoy yourself.

PAM

Well, okay. I guess it might be an opportunity to meet a new guy. Maybe someone who looks like Troy Donahue.

WINIFRED

And forget Kenny.

PAM

All right. Let's go. La ventura Roma!

Act II Scene 1

(The scene is a luxurious suite at the Rome Excelsior. Pam is sleeping in the bedroom with a pillow over her head. Jack enters from the sitting room.)

JACK

Come on, Pam. It's time to get up. The car and driver are coming at 10:30 to take us sightseeing. You've got to get ready.

PAM

I'm tired of sightseeing. You go. I'm staying in bed.
(Jack sits down on bed next to Palm)

JACK

Mother planned this trip for you. You can't disappoint her.

PAM

Yes, I can. I've seen enough - the Coliseum, the Pantheon, the Forum. Even that damn Trevi Fountain.

JACK

Today we're going to St. Peter's and then we're going to tour the Vatican. You want to see St. Peter's, don't you?

PAM

No, I don't. I miss Kenny and I hate Rome. The men are all short and comical acting.

JACK

You know we can stroll over to the American Embassy. It's right down the street from the hotel.
    And they have Marine Corpsmen guarding the Embassy.

PAM

(Pam rising out of bed) That sounds more interesting.

JACK

Maybe you can meet someone new to take your mind off Kenny.

PAM

I think you're right. Any ideas?

JACK

Aside from the embassy, not really, but let me think about it. We can go sightseeing now and stop off at the Embassy on the way home.

PAM

Oh, all right. Give me a few minutes to get ready.
(Jack walks into sitting room and dials a number.)

JACK

Hello, Mom. Listen, I must tell you, Pam is more depressed now than when we left Palm Beach. I have to force her to go sightseeing. Otherwise she'd stay in bed all day. If your idea was for Pam to meet some Italian lothario, it's not working out.
(There is a pause while Jack listens to Winifred.)
I'm glad you're enjoying your stay in East Hampton, but what am I going to do with Pam?
(Pause)
Let me see, do I know any classmates or fraternity brothers in Rome?
Pam asked me if I had any suggestions for her. You know, I'm thinking of someone and it might just work out. His name is David Henriques. I met him at Dartmouth in European History class. He's handsome and he exudes

self-confidence, which women apparently find irresistible. Believe me, he developed quite a reputation at Dartmouth.

(Pause)

Yes, I think he is the man who can end Pam's depression. So what if he is a ruthless seducer? This will be a fling, a rebound romance. They will probably never see each other again.

(Pause)

Okay, Mom, okay. I won't call you again unless I absolutely have to. Good-bye.

(Jack shakes his head and opens the Rome telephone book and searches for a number. He finds it and dials.)

Hello, David. It's Jack Foley from Dartmouth.

(Pause)

We met in European History class. Remember?

(Pause)

Yes, I'm here in Rome with my sister who is trying to get over an unhappy love affair.

(Pause)

(Jack chuckles.) Yeah, you're right. It is like something out of Henry James or Edith Wharton. Send your daughter to Europe to forget the guy who hurt her.

David, I think you can help her forget.

(Pause)

(Writing) Tomorrow morning at 11:00 on the Via Condotti in front of Hermes. Let's pretend it's a chance encounter. It's better that way.

Okay. We'll be there. See you tomorrow.

(Jack puts the phone down, stands up, and stares out at the audience. He scratches his head and rubs his chin.)

Gee, I don't know.

Act II Scene 2

(Scene. Front of curtain, walking along Via Condotti. Pam and Jack pass shops and a sidewalk cafe where they stop and chat.)

PAM

This is a lot like Worth Avenue. They've got a lot of the same stores here - Louis Vuitton, Bulgari, Ferragamo, Gucci. They're all here.

JACK

It's similar, but everyone seems younger and more formally dressed.
    (David Henriques appears, walking from opposite direction.)

DAVID

Jack Foley! I can't believe it! What a coincidence. This certainly is a long way from Dartmouth.

JACK

Great to see you, David. (They shake hands.) Say hello to my sister Pam.

Pam, this is David Henriques, a friend from Dartmouth.

DAVID

(His mouth drops. His eyes sparkle.)

Bella signorina.

(He bows low and kisses her hand. With his other hand he caresses her forearm.)

Oh, what skin! It's like velvet.

(He moves closer until they are almost touching.)

And your eyes, two emeralds in a crown of gold.

(He touches her hair.)

Like woven silk. Look at you. You're a blue sky, a sunlit day. You're joy. You're happiness. You're la dolce fa niente.

JACK

(Rolls his eyes. He seems at a loss for words. He looks at his watch.)

Well, I promised Mom I'd buy her a wallet at Gucci. She said Gucci in Rome is where all the Americans hang out. Why don't you sit here and talk for a while. I'll be back soon.

DAVID

(He leads Pam to a table and they sit.)

Jack never told me he had such a beautiful sister.

PAM

(She seems stunned by the whole experience.)
Do you - do you really think I'm beautiful?
And did you mean all that stuff you said?

DAVID

I said it, didn't I? So I must have meant it.

PAM

Nobody ever calls me beautiful in Palm Beach. Everyone there thinks I'm too large and heavy.

DAVID

This is Italy. We like our women full bodied. You remind me of a painting by Titian.

PAM

Whoa! I don't know how to respond to this. All my life I've been fighting a weight problem. In Palm Beach all the women are practically anorexic. Maybe I should move to Italy.

DAVID

I've been to Palm Beach. I know what you mean. I don't like that scrawny look. I like a woman with meat on her bones. Anyhow, why all this emphasis on looks!

PAM

That's Palm Beach! Appearances are everything. You know that.
   Well, tell me about yourself. Do you live in Rome?

DAVID

Yes. My family has lived here since the 16th Century.

PAM

But Henriques sounds Spanish. I thought you might be visiting Rome.

DAVID

No, no. Henriques is a Sephardic Jewish name. Originally we came from Spain.

PAM

Interesting. There are a lot of Jews in Palm Beach.
   In fact, almost forty percent of the population is Jewish.
   But I must be honest. I don't know many Jews.

DAVID

I've heard all the clubs there are restricted.

PAM

Some of them, but not all of them are.

Why, if your family has been here for 400 years, did you go to Dartmouth?

DAVID

You're changing the subject, but that's okay. My family are bankers. So I went to Dartmouth to study economics. I could have studied here, but my parents thought it might be a broadening experience. Besides, I also like to ski.

Are you a student?

PAM

I was a student at Palm Beach Community College. I have an Associate's degree in marketing. I know it sounds kind of lame.

DAVID

It sounds okay to me. You're always putting yourself down. Why?

PAM

Well, Jack is the smart one in the family. I guess I feel inferior to him.

DAVID

(He clasps her hands.) You seem intelligent enough to me. I see a lot of light in your beautiful green eyes.

PAM

I wish, I wish I'd met you sooner. I wish you lived in Palm Beach and I wish there were more men like you. There, I've made my three wishes!

JACK

(Jack appears.)

PAM

Hi, Jack.

JACK

I've just met a bunch of school friends at Gucci. I'm going to hang out with them for a while.

David, why don't you join us for drinks and dinner at the hotel?

DAVID

Sounds good to me! I accept.
    (Jack exits stage.)

DAVID

You know, Pam, I really don't understand you. You've got a lot going for you. You're a beautiful intelligent woman. Yet you seem insecure.

PAM

I guess I am insecure. David, I must be honest with you. Not everyone has such a high opinion of me. My mother is always after me to lose weight and she always compares me unfavorably, I might add, to Jack.

DAVID

Mother-daughter relationships are difficult. My sister has some of the same problems you do. Mothers want their daughters to be just like them.

PAM

You got that right! My mother is very petite and seems somewhat cold and reserved. I'm just the opposite.

DAVID

You can't live to please your mother. You have to become your own person. Find your own way and you will. I know you will.

PAM

What about you? Have you found your own way?

DAVID

For better or worse, I don't have to. My life is laid out for me, kind of like the Prince of Wales.

PAM

Oh, are you going to be king? (Both laugh.)

DAVID

Not exactly. The Henriqueses are private bankers and have been for generations. As the oldest son, I'm being groomed to take over as bank president when my father dies. I could rebel, of course, but I don't think I will.

We have a lot of tradition behind us. I remember my grandfather telling me about Largo 16 Ottobre 1943. Rome was occupied by the Germans. On that date the Nazis came to the Synagogue of Emancipation and demanded 110 pounds of gold. If the Jews didn't produce the gold within 24 hours, they'd be taken to concentration camps.

My grandfather donated 25 pounds and the total amount was raised, but some Jews still went off to concentration camps. So my heart and soul is here in Rome with my family and the bank.

But let's not get too serious. You're in Rome to enjoy yourself and see the sights.

(He looks at his watch.) But speaking of the bank, I have to go to work there now. I'll see you tonight.

Act II Scene 3

(Scene: Later that evening at hotel suite. She is tipsy and light-headed.)

PAM

Wow, what a dinner! I love this Roman cuisine, but I may have had too much wine.

DAVID

Why not? You're on vacation. You might as well enjoy yourself.

PAM

Oh, I am, I am. Ever since I met you I am. A.D., Anno Domino or is it Anno David, the year of David?
    Why aren't there more men in America like you?

DAVID

What are American men like? Obviously I've met a lot of them, but what are they like from your perspective?

PAM

They're not very romantic for one thing. Not at all, really, and they're very self-centered. All they seem to want to do is watch sports on TV. Baseball, football, golf, hockey, basketball, tennis. It's never ending!

DAVID

Soccer is our big sport.

PAM

But you don't watch it day and night, I hope!
(She looks at radio on table.) What we need here is a little music. (She turns radio on. *Al Di La* starts to play.)
Now, this is romantic! Let's dance. I remember this song from *Rome Adventure* with Troy Donahue and Suzanne Pleshette. That movie made me want to visit Rome.
(They start to dance. David holds her tight and she is obviously enjoying the dance.)
Now that's romantic! What does *Al Di La* mean?
(David translates and sings with the music and they continue to dance.)

DAVID

I did not believe I could ever say these words:
    "Beyond the limits of the world, that's where you are.
    "Beyond infinite time, beyond life.

"That's where you are, beyond everything, that's where you are for me."

PAM

That's what I call romantic!
(They dance out to the balcony.)
Here it is, Rome, the Eternal City! What's the expression? See Naples and die. See Rome and start living. Well, I want to start living.
(They walk back inside to the bedroom and kiss passionately. Slowly they sink to the bed as the lights dim.)

Act II Scene 4

(The next morning David, Pam and Jack are having break-fast at a sidewalk cafe on the Via Condotti.)

PAM

(With enthusiasm) Where are we going sightseeing today, Jack? I'm eager to start.

JACK

What a difference a day makes. Yesterday you didn't want to go anywhere. You just wanted to stay in bed and sulk.
(Jack and David exchange knowing glances which Pam observes.)

PAM

That was yesterday. What about today?

JACK

I thought we might do a day trip to Tivoli Gardens.

PAM

Sounds great. Are you coming, David?

DAVID

No. (Looks at watch) I've got to go to work, but maybe I'll catch up to you this evening.

PAM

(Notices smirking between David and Jack)
     I've got to find the ladies room. Will you excuse me for a second?
     (Pretends to go to ladies room, but hides behind pillar where she can hear David and Jack speak.)

JACK

(Jack and David high-five.) Way to go, David. I knew you were the man to get the job done. Mother will be pleased.

DAVID

Your sister is very beautiful, but I must say she was very eager. You'd better keep an eye on her. Rome is full of men preying on tourists - especially blond tourists.

JACK

I don't think it will be necessary. I think she only has eyes for you.

PAM

(returns) Having fun, boys? I hope you are because I don't find any of this amusing. So I've been set up by you two schemers. Well, I hope you're happy because I'm not.

David, I never want to see you again - ever!

And as for you, Jack, you're not my brother. You're a real shit!

DAVID

Excuse me. I've got to go to work. (exits)

PAM

How could you set me up like this and why didn't I realize it? Your friend David must have quite a reputation at Dartmouth. He sure had me fooled.

JACK

I was just trying to cheer you up. You seemed so downcast. I thought he could help you out of your depression.

PAM

I'll bet this was mother's idea.

JACK

She asked me if I knew anyone from Dartmouth who lived in Rome.

PAM

I can't even trust my own family.

JACK

We were just trying to help.

PAM

Thanks a lot! I don't need your help.
(They sit in angry silence.)

Act II Scene 5

(Taylor Carroll walks by the table. He is pale and thin with bad posture. He is dressed Palm Beach style with Gucci loafers, no socks, white trousers, and a pink Polo shirt. He wears dark glasses.)

TAYLOR

Jack Foley! I don't believe it, or do my bloodshot eyes deceive me!

JACK

Taylor Carroll, what are you doing here? You're dressed like you're still in Palm Beach.

TAYLOR

I'm here with a group of Palm Beach grande dames. My mother got sick at the last minute. So I filled in for her.

JACK

Doesn't sound so great! How's it going?

TAYLOR

So-so. I'm the only man. So the ladies all confide in me. All they do is gossip about the other ladies and tell me how much they despise them. Believe me, it gets old.

JACK

Women in groups! That's what Palm Beach is all about.
(Looks at Pam.)
    Oh, I'm sorry. My mistake. This is my sister Pam.
    Pam, say hello to Taylor Carroll.

PAM

Hi, Taylor. I've heard about you or maybe read about you in the shiny sheet. I thought you lived in New York and helped run the Hydra Mutual Fund.

TAYLOR

I used to, but the pressure was too great. The stockholders were driving me crazy. So I sold my shares and moved back to Palm Beach.

JACK

Where are you living?

TAYLOR

At home. My Dad died recently and my mom isn't feeling too well. So now at 35 I'm living at home again.

JACK

How do you like it?

TAYLOR

It's okay. I got my old room back. (They both laugh.)
Anyhow, my mom hoped some of these old gals on the trip would want to invest their money with me, and quite a few of them are interested. One of these days I'm going to start my own mutual fund, but right now I'm relaxing and taking life easy.

JACK

No more investing?

TAYLOR

I do some trading and manage my own account, but for the time being I want to concentrate on enjoying myself.

JACK

How's the market doing?

TAYLOR

Not so good. We keep having these Kennedy crashes. If the President would keep his mouth shut, the market would be fine.

JACK

Any stocks you'd recommend?

TAYLOR

Well, you can't go wrong with stocks like Eastman Kodak, Xerox, and Polaroid. Then there's always the bellweather General Motors.

JACK

What about IBM?

TAYLOR

Oh, I don't know. I wouldn't buy it in here. I think it's had its day.
(Looks at Pam)
You've been holding out on me, Jack. You never told me you had such a beautiful sister.

PAM

Oh, boy. Here we go again. In Palm Beach I'm a wallflower, but in Rome I'm the belle of the ball.

TAYLOR

(Seems surprised) Well, excuse me! Have you ever heard the expression, "The sign of a mature personality is the ability to accept compliments"?

PAM

Well, in that case I prefer to remain immature. I just finished a whirlwind fling with one of these Roman lotharios and he could really lay on the bullshit and I fell for it. So please, Taylor, don't make a pass at me because I'm not interested in having an affair with you or anyone else.

TAYLOR

You didn't have to come all the way to Rome to meet a lounge lizard. They're all over Palm Beach. You should try the bar at Taboo or the Leopard Room.

PAM

What's a lounge lizard?

TAYLOR

Oh, I don't know. He's a guy who hangs out in bars and tries to seduce women with flattery and oily charm.

PAM

Sounds familiar! Exactly like the guy who seduced me.

TAYLOR

There's a female version of the lounge lizard. Their sun-tanned leathery skin makes them look like lizards. They hang out in bars and try to seduce younger men.

PAM

That sounds a lot like Palm Beach. I'll bet you've logged a lot of hours in these gin joints, Taylor.

TAYLOR

A few. It's really hilarious. Most of the female patrons are gold diggers and the men are mainly lounge lizards. So not much happens. It's a standoff.
    By the way, what are you guys doing here?

JACK

Pam just had a bad experience with some guy. So Mom sent her over here to forget him.

TAYLOR

Sounds like something out of Henry James or Edith Wharton!

PAM

You're right about that, and you just heard what happened.

TAYLOR

It sounds like we're all here to forget something. I suggest we try to find a place that makes a really good Bloody Mary, the kind they make at the Bougainvillea Club.

PAM

How come I've never seen you at the club, Taylor?

TAYLOR

I guess you don't play tennis like your brother. That's how we met.

PAM

Golf is my game.

But don't you ever come to Sunday lunch? That's when most of the members are there.

TAYLOR

No, I'm usually too hungover and the noise at lunch is deafening. It's like being at a Florida-Florida State football game. Then by 2:30 everyone's gone and you could hear a pin drop. That's when I go for a swim and try to clear my head.

JACK

We're staying at the Excelsior. They cater to Americans. So they must be able to make a Bloody Mary.

TAYLOR

(Rising) If they don't know how, I'll show them. Let's get out of here.

Act III Scene 1

(The hotel suite three days later)

(Pam is talking on the telephone with Taylor while filing her nails. She seems bored.)

PAM

No, Taylor, I don't want to have dinner with you this evening. I'm still hungover from last night. Yes, I am looking forward to going to St. Peter's tomorrow.

(Door opens. Jack and David enter.)

PAM

(Surprised to see them) Yes, Taylor, I'll see you tomorrow at nine o'clock.

(Hangs telephone up)

(To David) What are you doing here? I told you I never wanted to see you again.

And, Jack, don't get me mad at you all over again.

JACK

Now, hold on, Pam. Take it easy, Pam. David just wanted to have a brief conversation with you. I'm going down to the bar.
(Jack exits.)

PAM

David, I don't see any reason to talk to you. We're finished. Whatever it was, it's over.

DAVID

I don't know. I can't stop thinking about you. I've been involved in other situations like this ...

PAM

I'll bet you have. You must have majored in seduction at Dartmouth because you sure are good at it.

DAVID

But usually I have very little feeling for the woman in-volved. This time it's different. I think I love you, Pam.

PAM

Oh, come on. Is this more of your Italian bullshit? Jack told me all about you, how you were the Don Juan of

Dartmouth, how nobody could resist you and how you always dumped these conquests quickly.

Well, I'm dumping you, lover boy. So you can move on to your next conquest.

DAVID

You don't believe me, do you, when I swear I have feelings for you I've never experienced before.

PAM

(Pretends to be playing a violin)

(David looks crestfallen. Pam softens.)

Look, there's no future for us. You told me your life is laid out for you and you're going to live it here in Rome. I don't speak Italian and I have no desire to move to Italy. I like Palm Beach and that's where I plan to live.

DAVID

(Pause) Is it because I'm Jewish?

PAM

Oh, come on. That has nothing to do with it.

DAVID

When we were talking about Jews in Palm Beach, you changed the subject. You didn't seem to want to talk about it.

PAM

I told you there are a lot of Jews in Palm Beach - about forty percent of the population. I just don't happen to know many. Our group sticks together. We're sort of like a clan. We belong to the same clubs, go to the same cocktail parties, travel in the same circles. It's kind of boring, now that you mention it.

But we all have the same values and appreciate the same things.

DAVID

Like what?

PAM

Well, you know Palm Beach. Money is number one. It's what Palm Beach is all about. If you don't have money, you don't belong here. Old money - new money - it doesn't really matter, but old is probably better. You hear a lot of talk about the nouveau riches - too showy, too vulgar - but that's Palm Beach. Displaying your money is okay whether it's old or new; huge homes, Rolls-Royces, Bentleys, Ferraris - you see plenty of them. Gaudy jewelry, brightly colored clothes, that's Palm Beach.

After money, socializing is probably number two; cocktail parties, dinner parties, art gallery openings, charity balls. If you're not social, there's no point in living in Palm Beach. Have I left anything out?

DAVID

I don't know. That's quite a list.

PAM

Oh, I've left out my bugaboo, slimness. Slimness is much admired and anorexia is everywhere. Bravo for the Italians; they seem to like buxom women.

But so what? You're not moving to Palm Beach and I'm not moving to Italy. So I don't think we have anything to talk about.

And whether you're Jewish or Buddhist or Confucian, it doesn't matter.

DAVID

I told you I could change my mind. I don't have to live in Rome. Maybe we could open a branch of our bank in Palm Beach.

(Pause) You know, that's not a bad idea.

PAM

(Sarcastically) Well, when you open your branch in Palm Beach be sure to look me up. Maybe we can talk then.

DAVID

(Pause) Maybe I can escort you around Rome while you're here. We don't have to be intimate. I know a lot of places you've probably never see.

PAM

I've already found an escort. Thank you.

DAVID

(Surprised) Who is he?

PAM

He's a nice boy from Palm Beach, he's older, 35, so we never met before. He used to run a mutual fund in New York. Now he's just taking it easy and enjoying life.

DAVID

Do you love him?

PAM

You're full of questions, aren't you? Let's say I'm working on it. He's someone who likes to drink, party, and have a good time. I'm okay with that. He's a member of the clan and he has the same traditional values. He's extremely eligible.

DAVID

I notice you didn't say he has the same values you have.

PAM

These are the same values my mother and the rest of my family cherish.

DAVID

So you're trying to please your mother again? You know you never will no matter how hard you try.

PAM

When you're young it's easy to be a rebel, but I don't know. If I want to live in Palm Beach, I guess I'll have to embrace these values and when I get older I'm sure that I'll want to.

DAVID

You don't seem very sure.

PAM

I'm not, but Taylor - that's his name - has a lot of good qualities. By Palm Beach standards, he's quite a catch. No, he's not as handsome and dashing as you. He's probably not as intelligent, but he's made a bundle of money and he'll probably make much more. My life is going to be easy. I can have anything I want.

DAVID

You mean material things, don't you? You know you haven't mentioned love. What kind of a relationship is this? You don't love him, but you're going to marry him. That doesn't make much sense to me. I tell you I love you, but you're not interested. Pam, I have to wonder about your values.

PAM

Oh, come on, David, this isn't fair. Your life is laid out for you and I just don't fit in.
(Turns away and tears come to her eyes.)

DAVID

You're crying. (Holds her in his arms and kisses her gently.) I don't fit in, you don't fit in; where does love fit into all of this?

PAM

I don't know. Everything has happened so quickly. I'm trying to sort it all out and you're not helping. Of course I want love, but I want security, too. I don't think I could ever trust you. You have quite a reputation, you know?

DAVID

Your reputation isn't the best, either.

(Takes her hands in his.) Look, with all these other women it was just a game, a challenge. You know, recreational sex. With you it's the real deal.

PAM

(Recovering her poise.) It's no use, David. I've got to learn to love Taylor. I know that sounds like a tired old cliche, but that's what I've got to do. Taylor fits in. That's the question you hear all the time in Palm Beach: Does he fit in?

DAVID

And I don't fit in?
     Over here in Rome I'm dashing, handsome, intelligent, and rich. In Palm Beach, I'd be just another Jew, albeit a rich one.

PAM

What a terrible thing to say! Times are changing and the members of these exclusive clubs are changing their ideas. Anyhow, you'd probably find these clubs boring.

DAVID

So I'd have to join all the Jewish clubs?

PAM

You'd probably find them more interesting. Anyhow, none of this is going to happen. I mean, I do sort of like you, but we have no future.

DAVID

So this is good-bye?

PAM

Yes. Just chalk me up as another conquest.

DAVID

You know, that is a very cruel thing to say.

PAM

I'm sorry. Well, not really. It's time to move on with my life and stop all this catting around, as my mother calls it.

DAVID

You sound so analytic and cold.

PAM

That's the way women are. There's a big misconception that we're romantic and men are sensible and down to earth. Well, men are the real romantics and women are hard-headed.

DAVID

Hard-hearted I would say.

PAM

Say whatever you want, but I'm going to marry Taylor. David, good-bye.
(Curtain)

Act III Scene 2

(The setting is the Foleys' living room. Pam has returned from Rome. She is talking with Winifred. It is the cocktail hour.)

WINIFRED

How does it feel to be back in Palm Beach, Pam?

PAM

I miss Rome already. At first I didn't like it, but now I can't wait until I return. I learned a lot over there and my self-confidence has soared.

WINIFRED

Wow, what happened?

PAM

Well, I met two men and both claim to adore me. Not bad, huh?

I don't know. Just being in Rome I felt a lot stronger, more myself.

WINIFRED

Maybe you should go back?

PAM

No. I want to stay in Palm Beach, but I must tell you, Mom - and you'll be proud of me - both these men are intelligent, well educated, attractive, and they both have background. One of them, Taylor Carroll, is the great grandson of the only Catholic signer of the Declaration of Independence.

WINIFRED

That should please your uncle.

PAM

And the other one is a private banker whose family has lived in Rome for 600 years.

WINIFRED

Wow! And here you went out with used car salesmen and ballroom dance instructors. I don't get it.

PAM

I didn't have the confidence to go out with men with class and intelligence. I felt they wouldn't like me. Let's face it. My self-esteem was very low. Now it's very high.

But I must tell you, Mom, there is a problem with these men.

WINIFRED

You don't mean . . .

PAM

Yes, I do. I'm expecting, Mom.

WINIFRED

Who's the lucky father?

PAM

I don't know.

WINIFRED

What do you mean you don't know? Don't tell me it was an immaculate conception?

PAM

No, I don't think so. I had sex with two men in Rome.

WINIFRED

Oh, my. And neither one used protection?
(Pam nods.)
I presume you had sex with David first, and then with Taylor?
(Pam nods.)
Is this catting around ever going to stop?
Keep it up and you'll really ruin your reputation.

PAM

Don't blame me, Mom. You and Jack set me up with this David character. Remember?

WINIFRED

Jack told me you were depressed. We both thought David would cheer you up. I didn't mean for you to have sex with him.

PAM

You know how these Italian men are. They prey on American women. David is an expert seducer, hard to - impossible really to resist. But it was just a fling. You know, Roman fever!

WINIFRED

I thought Roman fever was malaria - not sexual frenzy.

PAM

It may have been malaria in your time, but today it's sexual curiosity.

WINIFRED

Sexual curiosity seems to be the story of your life. Okay. So you had a fling with David. What about Taylor?

PAM

It's different with Taylor. He says he loves me and I think I'm in love with him.

WINIFRED

What do you know about this guy and why do you find him attractive?

PAM

I think you've probably read about him in the shiny sheet, Mom. He's from Palm Beach, but was living in New York managing a mutual fund, but he sold his shares in the fund and has moved back to Palm Beach.

WINIFRED

Well, he must have a lot of money. That's good.

PAM

Well, that's part of it. He's attractive, intelligent, good company. We have fun together. He does like to drink a lot, which worries me a little bit, but I think he can control it.

Taylor is very generous and if I married him, I could probably have anything I wanted.

WINIFRED

That all sounds good, but why didn't he use protection?

PAM

Because I thought it was my safe time of the month.

WINIFRED

I assume David didn't use protection, either, but Taylor doesn't know that.

So you can tell Taylor that David did use protection and, therefore, Taylor must be father of your child.

PAM

I'm not going to lie, Mom.

WINIFRED

Why not? Well, maybe you won't have to. If he's a true gentleman, he'll do the right thing and marry you. He has to take responsibility.

PAM

Oh, Mom. I don't want to beg.

WINIFRED

(Winifred sighs.) Pam, even after all your experience you don't understand men. They're all like little boys. You have to take them by the hand and lead them to the altar. Otherwise, nobody would ever get married.

PAM

I don't want a little boy. I want a man. I want a man who wants me and I certainly don't want to trap him.

WINIFRED

(Winifred heated) You don't want your child to be a bastard, do you?

PAM

That's a strong word, Mom. Many children today grow up without a father.

WINIFRED

But the father has to take responsibility. You must establish paternity to protect the rights of the child.

PAM

What do you mean? Who cares who the father is?

WINIFRED

The State of Florida cares. If you're not married, the State requires you to fill out a form acknowledging paternity. It's listed with Florida's Bureau of Vital Statistics and the father listed becomes the legal father.

PAM

How do you know all this?

WINIFRED

(Winifred sighs.) You remember Melinda Livingston? Well, she had an illegitimate child and her mother told me all about it.

But I don't want you to go through all this. Insist that Taylor marry you. He'll do it if you approach him correctly.

PAM

I told you, Mom, I don't want to beg.

WINIFRED

Asking isn't begging. Remind him of his responsibilities and you can also tell him that he'll never, ever, ever see his child unless he agrees to marry you. That should convince him.

You know, Pam, you'd better discuss this immediately with Taylor. I suggest you talk to him tomorrow.

Act III Scene 3

(The next day. Pam nervously sits in the Foleys' living room awaiting Taylor. She paces up and down. The door bell rings. Taylor walks in.)

Taylor

Hi, honey. (They kiss.)

PAM

(nervously) It's great to see you. I wanted to talk to you about something. Can I get you a drink?

Taylor

How about a martini?
    (Pam goes to bar and mixes a pitcher of martinis.)

PAM

    Come sit. (She pats a spot next to hers on the sofa. She sips her drink. Then with deliberation she places it on the coffee table.)

We certainly enjoyed ourselves in Rome, didn't we?

TAYLOR

We certainly did. I miss it already.

PAM

(Pam stares intently at Taylor.)
    I think maybe we had too much fun.

TAYLOR

I'm not sure I understand what you're saying.

PAM

I guess I'd better get right to the point, Taylor. I'm pregnant.

Taylor

(Seems surprised. Sips his drink.)
    I don't know what to say. Are you sure you're pregnant?

PAM

Positively. I missed my period and I have the usual symptoms of morning sickness and food cravings.

Taylor

(Pause) Well, what are you going to do about it?

PAM

I thought you might say what are we going to do about it.

Taylor

(Pause) You want me to marry you?

PAM

Yes, I do. I thought you'd feel the same way.

Taylor

(Rises and starts to pace.) This is kind of sudden, isn't it? I'll have to think about it.

PAM

For how long?

Taylor

I don't know. Look, I don't like all this pressure you're putting on me. Let's slow down and think this through. I know I should have used protection, but you said it was your safe period of the month.

PAM

I thought it was. If I didn't think it was safe, I would have insisted you use protection.

Taylor

So how come you got pregnant?

PAM

I don't know. These things happen.

Taylor

(Pause) You had sex with David before me, didn't you?

PAM

That was one night. You and I were together - I don't know - five or six nights. I'm almost positive you're the father.

Taylor

Well, if I married you, we'd have to do a pre-nup.

PAM

(Angrily) A pre-nuptial agreement! Those are for gold diggers. You think I'm only interested in your money?

Taylor

Look, I've got to protect myself. I'm worth millions now and expect to make more millions.

(Sarcastically) This is Palm Beach, remember?

You know there is something called abortion.

PAM

Go to hell, Taylor! I don't believe in it and I deeply resent you even suggesting it.

I wish your great-great grandfather, the only Catholic signer of the Declaration of Independence could hear this conversation. (Voice rising) If this is what you call love, I never want to see you again.

I thought you were a gentleman. I was hoping you'd be excited and want to do the right thing.

By the way, if it is your child, you know you'll have to take responsibility.

Taylor

You mean child support? I think I can afford it.

We did have a good time together and I guess I love you, but I'm not sure I want to marry you.

PAM

(angrily, leading him to the door) Well, then I guess we have nothing more to talk about.

(Slams door)

Taylor

(Knocking on door) Pam, Pam, wait a minute, will you?
Look, I do love you and I can't bear the thought of being without you.

PAM

(Pam opens door.) Oh, boy, you sure changed your tune quickly.

Taylor

Let's sit down and talk some more about this.

PAM

What's there to talk about? Either you want to marry me or you don't.

Taylor

Well, I'm not sure. You're still kind of young, aren't you?

PAM

I don't think so. I've always looked forward, ever since I was a little girl, to getting married. When I met you, I couldn't believe it. I thought you were my dream come true. And there you were in Palm Beach and we'd never met. So meeting in Rome seemed like we were fated for each other.

Taylor

I've got to admit I felt the same way, but getting married after such a short courtship? I just don't know.

PAM

We get along. We have a lot in common - marriage is always a roll of the dice, but I'm willing to take the chance. But look, if I have to sell you on the idea, then I'm not interested.

Taylor

Hold on a second. I didn't say I wasn't interested, but wouldn't you like to find out if the child is actually mine and whether we can have more children in the future? As you know, many couples today have trouble conceiving.

PAM

Suppose the child is not yours?

Taylor

I really think it is. Oh, all right, if we're going to do the testing, I guess I'll marry you even if it's not mine.

PAM

You're a real sport, Taylor.

But will the test endanger the baby's life?

Taylor

No, no, no. They don't stick any needles into you or anything like that.

PAM

Can this be done right away?

Taylor

I'm not sure, but I don't think so. I think you have to wait a couple of weeks.

PAM

Great! By then I'll be showing and everyone will be staring at me, asking questions.

Taylor

(He puts his arms around her.) Who gives a shit? Let's have another drink.

Act III Scene 4

(Two weeks later. Jack, Winifred, Lawrence and Pam sit in the living room. It is cocktail time.)

WINIFRED

I'm glad the whole family is together and we can discuss Pam's predicament. I've already told her to marry Taylor, but she seems to have some reservations.

JACK

Taylor comes from an old Palm Beach family. He has money. He's polite, well-mannered. He's eligible.

LAWRENCE

A true gentleman, that's the kind you have to look out for.

WINIFRED

What's that supposed to mean?

LAWRENCE

They're polite and well-mannered to your face, but behind your back they're sneaky. You can't trust them.

WINIFRED

Taylor said he'd marry Pam after the results of the test are in even if he's not the father.

LAWRENCE

It sounds to me he's looking for any excuse not to marry her. Otherwise he'd marry her now and not wait for the test results.

WINIFRED

What do you think, Jack?

JACK

I've played tennis with him a few times. Sometimes that tells you a lot about a person.

What sort of game does he play - power, consistent, straightforward, tricky?

Based on Taylor's game I would say he's honest, trustworthy and reliable, but he's a gambler. He doesn't play the percentages. He plays a power game. So he may have macho issues. The macho thing would work in your favor, Pam, because a child would reinforce Taylor's masculinity.

WINIFRED

Oh, my God! All this Ivy League psychology! What do you think, Lawrence?

LAWRENCE

I think he's a gentleman if he marries Pam. Otherwise he's a cad.

WINIFRED

I don't want to sound like someone out of the Stone Age, but I believe you should be married if you're having a child. I don't believe in children out of wedlock. I don't believe in abortion.

JACK

(Laughs and then speaks) Great, Mom! You'll be happy to hear a lot of Americans agree with you there.

But you forgot to mention premarital sex. How do you feel about that?

WINIFRED

I think you know the answer to that question.

JACK

Getting back to Taylor, did he mention abortion?

PAM

Yes, he did. And that's when I went bananas and threw him out of the house.

JACK

Even mentioning abortion shows a certain lack of sensitivity and perhaps he is trying to find a way out of marrying you.

WINIFRED

I think you should confront him again tomorrow and get a definite answer. You know there is another option. You could always have the child and put it up for adoption.

PAM

Absolutely not. It's mine and I'm going to raise the child.

LAWRENCE

You're going to raise the child all by yourself?

PAM

Why not? I guess I'll have to be mother and father.

LAWRENCE

Winifred, let's go out in the garden. (They exit.)

WINIFRED

The last time we talked in the garden you told me how much you admired me and how I was the woman you were always looking for. Do you still feel that way?

LAWRENCE

Yes, I do, and that's why I want to talk with you. Look, look, this is kind of hard to say and please don't laugh at me, but I'm getting kind of tired of being a professional escort and these women are all beginning to bore me.

WINIFRED

Mr. Palm Beach! Everyone's favorite extra man! I can't believe you're talking this way.

LAWRENCE

It's true, though. I guess I've been doing this for too many years and I'm tired of it. I think it's time for a change - a radical change.

WINIFRED

Oh, dear. I'm all ears.

LAWRENCE

(He moves closer to her, but hesitates.) Well, Pam is going to need help with the baby and I think the child deserves a real father - someone who's around all the time to help out and give guidance and, well, you know, I've missed out on being a father and this might be my last chance and, well, I think you know how I feel about you.

WINIFRED

Lawrence Foley, the confirmed bachelor, is this a proposal of marriage?

LAWRENCE

Yes, I guess it is.

WINIFRED

I think I'd better sit down. I don't think I can handle this.

LAWRENCE

Look, you don't have to give me an answer right now, but will you at least think about it?

WINIFRED

I'll think about it, but aren't you a little too old to be a father?

LAWRENCE

I don't think so. I'm healthy and in good shape. I think I can keep up with a child. Look, you and Pam are going to be around and there's probably going to be a nanny. It's not like I'm taking the responsibility all by myself.

WINIFRED

But we don't have to get married for you to play the father figure.

LAWRENCE

I know, I know. But as I told you, I'm tired of the social scene. Well, not completely.
    But I think if we're going to go to parties, I'd like you to be with me.

WINIFRED

But we still don't have to get married.

LAWRENCE

(Exasperated) Will you at least think about it?

WINIFRED

Okay, but for now I'm more interested in Pam getting married and her situation. Let's put our situation on hold.

Act III Scene 5

(The Foleys' living room the next day.)

WINIFRED

Pam, did you see the Shiny Sheet this morning?

PAM

No.

WINIFRED

Apparently after Taylor left here the other night he went to a bar, got drunk and crashed his car into a tree. He was arrested and charged with driving while intoxicated. He might lose his license.

PAM

Was he hurt?

WINIFRED

Yes. According to the paper, he broke his arm, bruised his ribs, and has facial lacerations.

PAM

Is he in the hospital?

WINIFRED

No. They released him.

He called this morning and said he would be coming over to see you later. I suspect he'll be here soon.

(Doorbell rings. Taylor enters with arm in sling and cuts on face.)

TAYLOR

Good morning, Mrs. Foley.

WINIFRED

How are you feeling?

TAYLOR

I'm in some pain, but it could have been worse. I'm lucky I'm still alive. Mrs. Foley, could I talk to Pam in private?

WINIFRED

Of course. Excuse me.
(Winifred exits.)
(Taylor sits on the sofa with some difficulty.)

TAYLOR

I've had a lot of time to think about us and I've decided I do want to marry you and we don't have to wait for the test results. I'd get down on one knee and propose except I'm in too much pain.

PAM

You changed your mind because you got drunk and totaled your car?

TAYLOR

I got drunk because I was very upset the other night. I've since changed my mind because I never get so drunk that I total my car. So if you can affect me that way it must be love.

PAM

I guess I should feel flattered, but I'm not. I've had a chance to think things over, too, and I've decided I'm not interested in marriage at this time.

TAYLOR

I don't get it. Last night you were practically begging me to marry you and now you're not interested.

PAM

A woman has a right to change her mind, you know. Don't take it personally, but I don't want to depend on someone else. I want to be my own person and discover life by myself.

TAYLOR

You told me in Rome we were well suited for each other.

PAM

I guess we are. That's part of the problem. I thought I might learn something about life when I got married. We're like two peas in a pod. Our backgrounds are too similar. Marriage with you would be a bore.

TAYLOR

Thanks a lot! You didn't think so when we were in Rome. You kept telling me about our similarities and how we were fated and all this other shit!

PAM

I think I was overstimulated being in Rome. Look, I want to be independent, learn about life, achieve success on my own terms - in real estate I might add. Maybe I'm just not ready for marriage and maybe I'll never be ready.

TAYLOR

(Sarcastically) Oh, boy. You want to be a modern woman.

PAM

Yes, I do. And you're about as traditional a man as I've ever met. I'm sure you want me to be a stay-at-home mom when the kids start arriving.
    I don't want to do that or be that kind of person.

TAYLOR

Maybe you don't want to live in Palm Beach.

PAM

I like it here. My family and friends are all here. I'm staying. Look, there are plenty of eager young things at the Bougainvillea Club. You shouldn't have any trouble finding what you want there.

TAYLOR

Maybe we should just give this whole thing some time. Let's think about it for a while. There's no real rush.

PAM

(Stands up.) I don't think so. My mind is made up. If I change it, I'll be sure to call you.
    (She leads him to the door.)

TAYLOR

Look, this isn't the end of us. I still want you and need you. I'm sorry, Pam. I'll always love you. (They embrace.)
    (Winifred comes down the stairs after hearing the door close.)

WINIFRED

How did it go? What did he say?

PAM

Now he wants to marry me without waiting for the test results?

WINIFRED

(Hugs Pam) Great! I'll start making plans for the wedding.

PAM

Don't bother. I told him I wasn't interested. I don't want to get married to him or anyone else - at least not right away.

WINIFRED

How could you? How could you? He seemed so right and he fits in so well.

PAM

Maybe that's the problem. Maybe I want someone more interesting - exciting - different.

WINIFRED

(Sags onto sofa holding her head.)
    What have I done wrong? Life guards, dance instructors, used car salesmen, this is excitement? With Taylor you could be happy and he'd give you anything your heart desires.

PAM

Except love.
    (Doorbell rings.)

VOICE OFF STAGE

Parcel Post. Sign here, please.

WINIFRED

It's for you, Pam. What's this all about?

PAM

There must be a card.

(She opens package and finds a card. She opens the card and reads aloud.)

"When I saw this emerald bracelet I thought of you because it matches your gorgeous green eyes. You said to be sure and look you up when we open a branch of Banca Henriques in Palm Beach. I'll be arriving shortly to finalize all details. All my love, David."

(Pam looks at Winifred, kisses the card, and shouts.)

Roma, ti amo! I can't believe it.
(She opens the box, puts on the bracelet, and admires it. She sits on sofa.)
Life sure is full of surprises.

WINIFRED

(She walks over to Lawrence, smiles at him, and takes his hand in hers, gazing into his eyes.)
It sure is.

THE END

Made in the USA
San Bernardino, CA
01 May 2017